RED GRASS

Also by Carter Travis Young:

RED GRASS

CARTER TRAVIS YOUNG

DOUBLEDAY & COMPANY, INC.
GARDEN CITY, NEW YORK
1976

All of the characters in this book
are fictitious and any resemblance
to actual persons, living or dead,
is purely coincidental.

Library of Congress Cataloging in Publication Data

Young, Carter Travis.
  Red grass.

  I. Title.
PZ4.Y68Re [PS3575.07]   813'.5'4
ISBN 0-385-11151-7
Library of Congress Catalog Card Number: 75-41678

76 001127

ONE

Through the late afternoon the rider climbed steadily, pushing because he knew he was close and he wanted—for no special reason that could be articulated—to be through the pass before nightfall. When he bedded down, he wanted to have had his first glimpse of the Antelope Valley, that was all. He wanted to carry that vision with him into sleep, to know that he was close.

Cullom Blaine wondered if Ned Keatch knew he was coming. If he could *feel* someone pressing close, as Blaine could feel Keatch near, almost as if he could smell him.

He hoped so. He wanted Keatch to know, to think about it, to wake sweating, his gut tight with fear.

As Samantha must have known what was coming, and waited for it.

The pass was not a cleft between two humps of rock or anything so clearly defined. The trail simply topped out, and over the rise there was a long, timbered shelf that sloped away gradually toward a vista of the valley far below. To the west, reaching above the timber line, the twin peaks of the Towers thrust into the cap of clouds.

The sun rode the shoulders of that granite range, and for a moment there was an odd illusion. The underside of the cloud layer glowed pink and crimson, and the floor of the valley below was blood red. Blaine, who was high enough to look out over much of the timber, stared at it. Then he saw the long shadows at the far end of the red valley, and he knew that what he had been tricked by was simply the last slanting rays of sunlight burning on the dry grass of the bottomland.

Dusk found him picking his way through a big stand of spruce and pines. When his shoulder brushed against a drooping branch, a cloud of needles drifted behind him. Dry, he thought. Dry as powder.

He made camp in a clearing among the trees. There was one big dark spruce whose lower branches sagged to the ground, creating a shelter almost like a tent. You couldn't see the sky, looking up through the branches. Underneath, there were the signs that showed where elk or deer had bedded down. Bears would even hibernate beneath such old trees, Blaine knew. It was very tall and old, and he respected it. He made a small fire, well away from the spruce or any other trees, and when he had had enough coffee he threw the dregs on the fire and finally kicked some dirt over it to put out the last embers. The night was cool in this high country, even in August, but he could do without the warmth of his fire on this one night. Might just as well throw a match into a powder keg as let sparks fly among these trees.

Once the sun went down and pulled its blood-red cloak after it, the valley had looked green enough in the far distance. But from what Blaine had heard, and what he could now observe, the grass on the floor would be brown and dry, like the brush that spread prickly and brittle over the foothills or the dry timber on the higher slopes. There had been two consecutive seasons of long, hot, unnaturally dry summers, and this land was in trouble.

Blaine had been five weeks on the trail, riding steadily each day, since he had first heard the rumor about Ned Keatch's whereabouts. His buckskin was footsore and tired, needing rest, and the ache that permeated Blaine's bones made him sympathetic. Well, it was almost over, this long ride.

It was possible, of course, that the grinding journey, like

so many others these past two years, would have been for nothing. The rumor about Keatch might have been false, or it might have had the name of the valley and the town center wrong, or it might have come to Blaine's ears too late, so that he would arrive long after Keatch had moved on.

But there had been a logic to the story that gave Blaine hope. The entire Antelope Valley was a powder keg, threatened not only by the danger of fire, which Blaine had sensed, but by the equally explosive and mindless fury of a range war. No one could tell him how the feud had started—often the participants themselves would be vague on such a matter, Blaine knew, and would little care once the bloodletting started—but the valley had been torn into opposing camps. The main street of Rush City, it was said, was a battle line, with hostile parties on either side.

And quick guns facing each other.

They always came when such a war threatened. The quiet, cold-eyed men with their well-oiled Colts and Winchesters. One would be hired first, and the other side would answer by putting out the call for its own gunman. Others would follow, and sooner or later there was the inevitable gunplay. What would have been a Saturday night brawl under other circumstances would become another excuse for reprisal and counterreprisal, and the hiring of more guns.

Ned Keatch's gun had been for hire in more than a dozen places that Blaine knew of. A range war lured men like him. It was a good place for him to draw high wages—and to hide.

One trouble was that Blaine had only the vaguest description of Keatch. Its terms would fit a hundred men, or a thousand. Slim, narrow-faced. A high-pitched voice. Sandy hair. Popeyes, but there was disagreement about their color. A gun hand that moved "like greased lightning." Not enough to pick Keatch out in a crowd.

Blaine would know him when he looked into his eyes. The

problem might be to get that close without drawing the lightning.

*   *   *

Blaine woke suddenly. He didn't know exactly what had warned him, but he did not stop to pin it down. He rolled out of his blanket, at the same time digging for his single-action Army Colt. He had used his saddle as a pillow, and the gun was in its holster hooked over the saddle horn.

"Pull it and you die!"

Blaine's hand froze on the walnut grips.

There was a moment when no one moved or spoke. Blaine was on the ground in the shadow of the big spruce, and the low, sheltering branches screened off much of the clearing where he had built his fire that evening. He wondered if the man who had warned him could see him clearly enough to know that his hand was on his gun, or if he had simply anticipated what Blaine's first move would be. Either way it didn't seem to matter. Blaine could see the stumps of perhaps a dozen pairs of legs out beyond the drooping skirts of the spruce.

"Go ahead," the same voice drawled. "Be a shame to disappoint St. Peter when he's got the gates wide open."

Blaine eased his hand away from the Colt and sat up slowly. "Expect he might have a few questions to ask before he opens those gates so wide," he said.

One of the men in the clearing chuckled.

"Come on out, stranger," the spokesman commanded. "Hands and knees will do fine. Does a man good to learn how to crawl."

There were a few more chuckles as Blaine emerged from the shelter of the spruce into the open. He saw the shapes of eight or nine men surrounding him, rather than the dozen he had guessed at first glimpse of all those boots. Each man carried some kind of iron, and each muzzle was pointing at Blaine.

He started to rise. A big man, square-shouldered and tall, thumbed the hammer of a six-gun. "Nobody told you to get up," he said. The voice was the same one that had barked the first warning.

Blaine stopped, still on one knee. "Nobody has to," he said quietly.

The clearing was suddenly very quiet. No one moved. Somewhere nearby a horse shifted weight, and the rubbing of saddle leather was clearly audible.

The tall man's shoulders lifted and fell in a shrug. "Your choice, pilgrim. If you're in such a hurry to talk your way through them gates—"

"No," Blaine cut him off. He could feel the tension at the back of his neck, and his jaw was set in a hard, stubborn line. "If you want to gut-shoot an unarmed man for standin' on his own two legs, that's *your* choice."

Very deliberately he pushed to his feet.

For a moment the stillness in the clearing held, as if no one breathed, each man waiting. Then the square-shouldered leader of the group stepped quickly toward Blaine, shoving his six-shooter forward until the end of the long barrel rammed against Blaine's hard belly. "Damn you, I warned you—"

"Hold it, Clete! You can't—"

"Shut up!"

There was barely controlled fury in the tall man's voice, but as he spoke to the other waddy his body heeled in that direction, and the movement pulled the muzzle of the six-gun with it. Blaine acted. In one motion he slid inside the gun, slapped one hand down on the taller man's wrist, and brought up his leg. The gunman was caught by surprise. His arm came down across Blaine's thigh like a stick meant to be broken. There was a sharp gasp of pain. The bone didn't break, but the gun skidded free, dropping from lax fingers to the ground.

Blaine hurled Clete from him and dived for the gun.

A shot exploded close to his ear, and a tongue of flame leaped toward his outstretched hand.

Blaine stopped his dive, his reaching hand only a foot from the gun on the ground. He didn't know which of the other men had fired, but the shot had clearly been meant to stop him, not to kill. It was a message Blaine understood instantly. Very carefully, he drew back.

He was still in a crouch when there was a rush of movement behind him. He started to turn but he was too late. The man called Clete launched a boot directly at his head. Blaine had time to make a half turn, so that the kick didn't catch him flush on the head. It slapped one ear and rammed squarely into Blaine's collarbone. He went down with his ear burning and his shoulder hot with pain.

He was aware of a blur of movement around him, scuffling, an angry curse. He was on his back, helpless as a beetle, when the tall man scooped up his gun and whirled toward him.

"Don't do it, Yeager!"

"No man puts me down—"

"Miss Roark won't stand for killin' a man when his hands is empty!"

Whatever the significance of that warning, it was enough to cut through Clete Yeager's rage. He stopped, the gun in his hand pointing at Blaine's chest. His glare flicked back and forth from Blaine to the other speaker. For the first time Blaine noticed that the Winchester in the second man's hands was pointing not at Blaine but at Yeager. Yeager saw it too.

He hesitated for another second, then abruptly drew back and holstered his six-gun. He turned from Blaine to glare at the man with the Winchester.

"Don't try to stop me another time, Walden," he said. "And don't ever point a gun at me again."

"Sure thing, Clete," Walden said easily. "But you got to admit you give him better'n he gave you. Let it end there."

Ignoring the comment, Yeager glared around the circle of silent men. "Get him on his horse," he said curtly. "We're takin' him to the ranch."

"Mind tellin' me why?" Cullom Blaine asked quietly.

Clete Yeager swung to confront him. Even in the darkness Blaine could see the cold glitter in his eyes. "You'll find out," he snapped. "And if you're what I think you are, you'll wish nobody stopped me from killin' you quick and easy."

He turned on his heel and stalked out of the clearing.

*　*　*

The column rode easily, cutting through stands of timber and open meadows where the dry, yellow grasses crackled underfoot, heading for a high table to the west. As the sky shaded from its deep purple to a pre-dawn gray, Blaine was able to see the men he rode with more clearly, and to note that, even when the line thinned out where the horse trail narrowed, there were always at least two men behind him.

Clete Yeager led the way. This dry land was dusty, and Yeager wasn't the kind to eat another man's dust. He was the kind that, on a cattle drive, you would always find riding point. Gunfighter by the look of him, and a confident one. There was always an unmistakable arrogance about such men. Power in those squared-off shoulders that gave him the appearance of having a board stuck up under his shirt. A dark, saturnine look, with black hair and thick black eyebrows, a long sharp nose, a cruel mouth. Most men who met him on a boardwalk, Blaine thought, would take care to step aside.

After a while the man called Walden fell in beside Blaine. He had seen a few more years than most of the others. His beard was salt-and-pepper, and the hair that ringed his rain-streaked Stetson was iron-gray. His eyes were brown and mild, like his voice, but Blaine didn't let that deceive him. Walden would be a hard man to buffalo. It had taken real nerve to call Clete Yeager off.

A gunman? Hard to say. Certain there were at least a half-dozen hard cases in this crew, in addition to Clete Yeager. But at the same time any outfit, even one caught up in a range war, was bound to have some cow punchers in it, men who were more likely to use a six-shooter to hammer nails or ventilate tin cans than to fire in anger. Walden, unlike Yeager and some of the others, didn't advertise what he was.

Ned Keatch wouldn't put up a sign, Blaine thought, especially if he knew he was being hunted. But Walden wasn't his man. Keatch's kind of meanness didn't need a sign.

Walden broke a long silence. "Don't remember what you said your name was."

"Never said."

"Uh huh." Walden clucked as if Blaine's reply were revealing. After a while he said, "Guess it don't matter much what a man calls hisself around these parts. I reckon if you taken a poll, you wouldn't find more'n one true name in ten."

"I never said," Blaine answered tersely, "because I wasn't ever asked before you nine brave men pulled iron on me."

Walden glanced at him mildly, but he said nothing.

They rode out of timber, black in this early light, and dropped down an open slope to another shelf. Some cattle stood somnolently on the table, watching the column of riders vaguely. They were lean, Blaine thought, but a long way from starving out. Two dry summers had meant poor pasture, but there was still enough to get even a big herd through. Drought might have contributed to the hostilities in the Antelope Valley war, but it wasn't the only reason, unless poor run-off had shriveled all the streams and dried up the springs. Cattle and men could go hungry for a while. They couldn't go without water.

"Blaine," he said, as if there had been no pause since his last words. "They call me Blaine."

Walden's glance was quick. "Would that be Cullom Blaine?"

"It would." Blaine looked at the older man sharply, but Walden was staring straight ahead. When it became clear that he wasn't going to add anything, Blaine said, "We've never met."

"No," Walden said softly. "I doubt I'd have ever forgot it if we had."

Blaine was not surprised. Wherever he rode now, there were men who had heard of the shootout with Abe Stillwell in the street in Fort Smith, or of his reckless invasion of Price's Landing, a notorious outlaw hangout down in Texas where he had gone in search of one of Ned Keatch's partners. The stories dogged him, making his hunt more difficult. He wondered if Walden would spread the word. Again, he could not be sure. Walden seemed a tight-lipped sort, not the kind who eagerly sought a hearing, gaining importance with the gossip he carried.

In the end it wouldn't matter. Blaine would do what he had come to do. Whether it came hard or easy made no difference.

Clete Yeager had been looking back at them, swiveling in his saddle. Now he said, "You two through holdin' your prayer meeting back there?"

"Passin' the time, Clete," Walden called out cheerfully. "Just passin' the time."

He grinned as Yeager showed his back. Blaine read the grin and said, "Yeager ramrod this outfit?"

There was so long a silence that he thought Walden was going to ignore the question. Finally Walden said, "He does now."

"Everybody else jump to his tune quicker'n you?"

Walden glanced at him, and Blaine thought he saw something sardonic in his gaze. But all he said was, "A man hires on, he'd best know who's givin' the orders, or he'll find more trouble than a sheepherder at a cattlemen's ball."

"That don't mean he has to crawl."

Walden chuckled. "Guessed you didn't much cotton to crawlin' from under that spruce." He grew thoughtful. "You took a long chance, Blaine, jumpin' Yeager when he was holdin' a gun on you. I doubt any man ever got away with that afore. He won't forget it."

"I don't want him to."

The two men fell silent, for neither was the kind who needed to fill up every space with talk. Blaine figured that he wouldn't get much more hard information from Walden. In any event, he was not as surprised by his hostile reception as he had let on. People in this valley would be jumpy and suspicious over any stranger's arrival until they knew who he was and where he stood.

One fact interested Blaine. Walden had used a woman's name to stop Clete Yeager in the clearing, warning against a cold-blooded killing. That seemed to suggest that Blaine might hope to get a fair hearing from Miss Roark.

He was speculating over what kind of woman it was whose name could have that effect on a stiff-backed gunman like Clete Yeager when the trail curled around a thin stand of cedar, climbed a short slope, and came into view of the clustered buildings of a ranch, low dark shapes of weathered wood at the far end of a grassy table. The shapes took on detail swiftly as the riders drew closer under the pale-blue wash of early morning sky.

"There she is," Walden murmured. "The Rocking Chair."

"Would the R stand for Roark?"

"You'll find out soon enough." There was a glint in Walden's eye that Blaine could not read.

A small stream wriggled along the south side of the table at the base of timbered hills. It angled across the meadow at one point, and the riders forded it. The water was shallow, hardly more than a trickle. Spring-fed, Blaine guessed, and a trickle like that would quickly run aground, but it explained

why much of this meadow was a richer green than the lower
valley, which, stretching below the table to the north and
east, was uniformly bleached of its color.

As the light grew and the pace of eager horses quickened,
the line of riders fanned out into a looser group, and Blaine
was able to make a more careful scrutiny of the men escort-
ing him toward the ranch. All but one or two had the flint-
eyed, hard-mouthed look of hired fighters rather than
cowmen, but he didn't see one who answered the meager
description he had of Ned Keatch.

But there would be others in the Rocking Chair's crew. A
few of them were visible now, stumbling out of the
bunkhouse or smoking the day's first cigarette while they
leaned against a corral railing and watched the approaching
riders.

Blaine felt a familiar tightening in his gut.

But the first thing he noticed when he rode into the yard
was the woman on the long porch of the main house. And
nothing in Walden's eye or Clete Yeager's manner had
prepared him for Kate Roark.

Standing at the top of the porch steps, one hand on a
square pillar, she seemed taller than she actually was. She
wore jeans which had shrunk to fit and looked as if they
might have to be peeled off, from the way they clung to full
hips and rounding thighs. A faded blue man's shirt pulled
almost as tight across her bosom, giving it a shape it had
never had on any man. Gaps threatened to open between
the two top button sets. High-heeled boots and a thick
crown of chestnut hair added to her illusion of height. Even
her stance, proud and somehow arrogant, made her appear
taller. Blaine guessed that she was quite well aware of her
appearance, and of the gaping stares she received.

But a number of the men in the yard were studying him
rather than the woman as he was escorted toward the
porch.

The woman eyed Blaine speculatively for a long moment

before she spoke, addressing Yeager. "What do you have there, Mr. Yeager?"

"Picked up a stray, Miss Roark." Yeager's glance flicked toward Blaine. "Found him hidin' under a tree over near the south pass. Looked like he didn't want to be seen, so I figured we should flush him out before he could sneak up on us."

Blaine smiled thinly at this description of his night camp. Kate Roark, whose eyes were very clear and alert despite the earliness of the hour, saw the reaction. "He could have been riding through," she said crisply.

"Not likely," Yeager said. "Not the way he was holed up."

The woman met Blaine's gaze openly. Those blue eyes were a striking combination with the rich darkness of her hair, a combination as Irish as her name, Blaine thought. What surprised him, once he began to get over the startling impact of her handsome face and figure, was that she was a young woman, perhaps no more than two or three years come of age. Young to command such deference from this crew of rough punchers and rougher gunmen. Even Clete Yeager used a different tone when he spoke to her.

"I'm Kate Roark, and this is the Rocking Chair," she said coolly. "You got anything to say for yourself, stranger?"

"Just wonderin'," Blaine said, "if this is always your way of welcoming strangers."

Clete Yeager jerked toward him. "Hold your tongue—"

"Be quiet, Clete," Kate Roark said sharply. "I asked him a question."

She studied the man on the buckskin more closely. His voice had rumbled quietly from a deep chest, surprising her. He was a bigger man than you took him for at first glance. It was hard to judge the height of a man in the saddle. That, and his relaxed posture, were deceptive. Although he wasn't heavy, there was an unexpected breadth of shoulder and an impression of hard muscles amply filling his shirt sleeves.

Hard suited the man, she thought. That face. You could strike a match on it.

She was also intrigued by the impression of rock-steady calm she sensed in the man. Anyone who could remain so much at ease in his present situation interested her. Then her curiosity increased when she realized that it wasn't *calm* she sensed in him, but something else, something . . . banked. As if there were a wildness inside that you couldn't see, held under tight rein. Like the wildness in her that her father had feared. . . .

She cut off the thought. Her tone was still sharp when she said, "You were found on Rocking Chair land. What reason did you have for being there?"

Blaine shrugged. "Never heard of it before this morning. It just happened to be on the way."

Kate Roark's face tightened. It was less pretty then, and there was a challenge in the blue eyes. "Maybe you're looking to find Brad Simmons then."

"Never heard of him either."

"You don't volunteer much information."

"No."

"Damn it, it's plain enough," Clete Yeager broke in. "This is no cowpoke, nor any kind of saddletramp. He's a high-line rider if I ever seen one, and if he didn't come to throw in with us then he's one of Simmons' bunch of lead throwers. Let me run him out—"

"I'll tell you what to do when I'm ready," Kate Roark said, so curtly that Yeager colored visibly under the weathered dark of his face. "And watch *your* tongue when you're talking to a lady."

Yeager opened his mouth as if he were going to reply, then closed it. He was angry, but not angry enough to challenge Kate Roark's authority. Blaine wondered why. A man like Yeager wasn't afraid of anyone, and any man he worked for would have to handle him on a loose lead. Kate Roark didn't bother, and Yeager took it from her. There had to be a reason.

Blaine could think of one, but he didn't see much point in speculation.

"There's a war on in this valley," the woman said to him. "When you know that, you know why we don't like strangers on Rocking Chair land." A smile seemed to lurk at the corners of her full mouth. "Especially close-mouthed strangers."

Blaine nodded briefly, as if this explanation were reasonable enough.

"I have your word you haven't hired on to Simmons or any of the other range jumpers hereabouts?"

"I already told you. I never heard of Simmons."

She eyed him thoughtfully for another moment. "No, you wouldn't lie, would you?" she murmured, as if thinking aloud. Abruptly she came to a decision. "You'll have to excuse our inhospitality. My father wouldn't let me hear the end of that, if he were alive. Rest your horse and come inside. Walden, see that buckskin gets fed and watered."

"Yes, ma'am."

Clete Yeager swung down from his bay. "You can take care of mine while you're at it," he said, starting toward the porch.

"That won't be necessary, Mr. Yeager," Kate Roark said coolly. "I don't need protection."

Yeager stopped as if he had been struck. A white line appeared around his mouth. A sudden fury in his eyes, he turned away from the woman, as if he didn't dare let her see it. It found a target in Cullom Blaine, but there was nothing he could do. Or would do, in the face of her clear decision to put him in his place.

Balefully he watched Blaine swing down and step onto the porch. In the doorway Kate Roark turned to look at Blaine. She smiled. "You haven't told us what to call you, Mr. . . . ?"

Blaine was aware that every man in the yard within earshot was listening. His answer came clearly. "Blaine," he said. "Cullom Blaine."

Then, not looking back, he followed the woman into the house.

TWO

Kate Roark regarded Blaine with amusement across the table. "More coffee, Mr. Blaine? Or shall I have Maria fry you a few more eggs?"

"No, ma'am," Blaine said, gulping down a mouthful before he spoke. "That is, no more eggs or I'll start to cackle. But I could use some more coffee."

"To wash it all down?"

"Yes. That is . . ." He stopped, wondering when was the last time he had felt his tongue getting tied up in this way. It was one thing to look at Kate Roark in the open, quite another to be alone with her in this room. He was silent as she poured more coffee into his cup, ignoring hers.

"I've seen starving wolves didn't act so hungry," she commented with a smile. The smile softened more than her words. It relaxed her face, letting the youthful beauty shine out. It showed a sparkle in her eyes, and let him see the softness of her lips.

"It's been a long spell since this wolf ate so well," he said with a comfortable sigh. "A man on the trail doesn't sit down to a feast every morning."

"I suppose not." She paused. "Has it been a long ride, Mr. Blaine?"

"Always seems long, if you look back."

"So you don't look back, you just look ahead." She did not wait for a comment. "I don't mean to pry, but . . . you don't seem like a drifter. A sun chaser, perhaps. But that isn't why you came to Antelope Valley, is it?"

"No."

Abruptly she laughed. Rising from the table, she said, "You'll tell me if you want to, and not before. Bring your coffee with you, Mr. Blaine. We might as well be comfortable."

The dining table filled one end of the long narrow room. The rest of the room was comfortably supplied with elegant furniture, imported from the East or from Europe. A huge stone fireplace dominated the long inner wall. There were hunting trophies above the long mantelpiece—a deer with an impressive spread of antlers, an elk and a moose, the white shaggy head of a bighorn. Blaine settled into a leather chair, holding his cup and saucer awkwardly. It was a man's room, he thought, in spite of the curtains over the bank of windows facing the porch. Kate Roark didn't go in for frills and lace, any more than petticoats, to judge by her shirt and jeans. But the room was not hers, he judged. She had apparently left it the way it was after her father's death.

"I'll bring you a mug," she said. "You look as if you're afraid you'll break that cup."

"That's all right," Blaine protested feebly.

She took the cup and saucer from him and returned a moment later with a heavy crockery mug of hot coffee. Blaine sighed, wondering where another swallow of anything would fit. When Kate Roark turned away, he caught a faint scent from her, of perfume or perhaps only the fresh sweet smell of a woman. His mouth felt dry and he took a swallow of coffee, burning his tongue.

She took a chair facing him.

Blaine said, "You spoke of your father."

"I wondered when you'd get to that."

"He passed away?"

"He was killed, Mr. Blaine! Shot down by one of the hired guns of Brad Simmons and his Cattlemen's Association. You might as well hear it, if you're going to be in this valley for long, and it's my guess you will be. There's been trouble for two years—it's been dry longer than that, as you can see for yourself, but the trouble was here even before the drought. That just gave them an excuse. My father, Sean Roark, was the first rancher to settle in this valley, and he made the Rocking Chair the biggest spread around. He came here when most people didn't think you could raise cattle in this high country. He proved you could, and then all the others, the scoffers and the claim jumpers and the ones who hadn't the sand or the brains to do it first when the stakes were high, then they moved in. They thought they could settle wherever they pleased, using the water we'd used from the beginning, taking the graze that was ours."

Blaine was silent, hearing the passion in the young woman's voice, the grief that wouldn't go away. It was something he could understand more than most.

"Brad Simmons used to be a friend, or we thought he was before we learned better. We grew up together. He—" She broke off, her lips curling in a bitter twist. "When trouble kept coming, they banded together, the smaller ranchers, claiming rights they never had. My father was a stubborn man, Mr. Blaine, but he was fair, and he fought fair. It was the others started hiring gunmen. Simmons sided with them. He's the leader now—every pack of coyotes has to have a leader. One of those hired killers drew on Pa, and . . ." She stopped, looking away. When she continued her tone was flat, hardened against emotion. "He was a fighter, Mr. Blaine, but he was no hand with a gun, and Simmons knew it. They forced a fight on him, knowing that he wouldn't back down even if he had no chance to win. And . . . he was killed. I call it murder, Mr. Blaine."

When she faced him again, Blaine was surprised to see that, although her eyes were bright, there were no tears. "I see," he murmured.

"No, you don't. You didn't know him. But you can know this about me, Mr. Blaine. I'm a Roark, and I swore I'd see them all buried, every one who sided against him. I've got my own hired guns now, and that's the way it is. You'd best know that, if you mean to be around here, whatever your reason." She paused, and the room was silent. Blaine heard the steady ticking of a pendulum clock against the far wall, and the sounds of Kate Roark's breathing. Finally she said, quieter now, "I doubt it'll work, Mr. Blaine."

"What's that?"

"You being here, and not taking sides. You'll have to choose."

Blaine shook his head. "I'm lookin' for a man. I heard there was trouble in this valley, and that he might be in it."

"He's quick with a gun?"

"That's what they say."

"Then he could be here." She paused. "He could be one of my crew."

"Maybe."

"I can't spare a man, Mr. Blaine."

Blaine's voice was soft, but there was something unyielding in it, implacable. "If he's here, you'll have to."

Kate Roark studied him for a long moment. "You can say that, knowing I can have twenty men in this room in a minute if I just yell? And you not even wearing a gun?"

"Yes."

Kate Roark stared at him, wondering. She thought now that she recognized what was banked inside him. She understood because the same hot fire burned deep in her: hate. "What's this man's name?" she asked.

"Ned Keatch."

She considered the name thoughtfully before she replied. "I've heard of no such man. He's not on my payroll, Mr. Blaine."

"I doubt he'd be usin' the same name."

She was silent a moment before she said, "You must have good reason for hunting him."

"Yes." That was all Blaine would say. The reason was not something he would trot out on request.

"When you find him, I don't suppose it will be his day for rejoicing." When Blaine said nothing, Kate continued to stare at him, as if considering what she would say next. The words, when they finally came, surprised him. "If I could guarantee to you that this Ned Keatch isn't part of the Rocking Chair crew, would you hire on with me, Mr. Blaine? Before you answer, think on it a minute. If Keatch isn't here, he's working for Simmons and the Association. Has to be, if he's the kind of man you say. If you work for me, sooner or later you'll find Keatch. Meanwhile, you'll do me some good." She paused, hesitating before she added, "I can use a good hand, Mr. Blaine. Especially the kind of man who doesn't quake when Clete Yeager speaks."

"How would you guarantee Keatch isn't working for you?"

"You'd recognize him if you saw him up close?"

Blaine thought of the sketchy descriptions he had of Keatch, but he didn't hesitate. "Yes, I'd know him."

"Then you just give the word and I'll line up every man on the Rocking Chair for you to look at!"

Blaine took his time before replying. The offer was certainly tempting. Kate Roark herself was part of the reason. Even more importantly, she was holding out a quick chance to eliminate half of the assorted gunslingers and badmen who had been drawn to the Antelope Valley War from his search. If Keatch wasn't with the Rocking Chair, Blaine's hunt could turn elsewhere, and much time would have been saved.

But there was a rub. If he agreed to her terms, he would no longer be free to hunt on his own. He would be fighting her war, and it had nothing to do with him.

His answer, when it came, was blunt. "No, Miss Roark. I can't let you tie my hands that way. I have to go my own way."

She felt anger rising. She was unaccustomed to having anyone say no to her in any way, to say nothing of having the refusal voiced with no attempt to soften it. "Are you so sure I'll let you?" she said sharply.

"Don't pay to be too sure of anythin'," Blaine said. "But I think you will."

Kate Roark felt the dark flush that rose to her neck. It was as if the hard, unyielding core in this man challenged *her*. Since Sean Roark died there had been no one to balk any turn of her will. No one had looked at her as this man did, flatly stating what he meant to do, regardless of what she wanted.

She rose suddenly. When she spoke, Blaine heard the arrogance and haughtiness she had used on Clete Yeager in the yard, and the unvoiced anger as well. "I'll ask the men to take you into town, Mr. Blaine. You'll not hunt your man in my bunkhouse. What you do in town, or anywhere else except the Rocking Chair, is your own business. But if you go up against one of my men, I don't care who it is, I can't answer for what will happen. Clete Yeager won't likely believe it's just a personal matter, and we should just look the other way."

"It doesn't much matter what he believes," Blaine said, and she heard in his voice the rock hardness she saw in his face.

"Nor what I believe?" she retorted. But she didn't wait for an answer.

At the door Cullom Blaine faced her, standing close. Their proximity brought a tightness to his breathing, an ache he had not felt in two years, one that he had thought forever buried. The knowledge that it was not angered him, for it seemed disloyal, even dishonest.

He said flatly, "I'll want my gun. One of your men has it."

Her gaze met his directly. Her blue eyes were cold, deny-

ing the mutual attraction he had sensed. "Yes, you'll need it,
I expect."

When he stepped off the porch into the bright sunlight,
he was thinking of Samantha.

THREE

Walden was one of those who rode into Rush City with Blaine, along with Clete Yeager and a half-dozen other hands. They pulled up on a bluff that overlooked the brick and clapboard buildings of the town. The town had been built between this bluff and a gentler hill to the north, where many of the houses climbed the slope. The trail which Blaine and the Rocking Chair escort had taken circled down from the heights and straightened out to become the main street of the town, heading due north. The flat bottomland of the valley opened out to the west, and a riverbed meandered across it. From here it looked dry. Even the narrow line of growth flanking the stream on either side appeared more gray than green. The whole bottom of the valley was a dust bowl. Everything that moved kicked up a cloud behind.

Blaine wondered if a good rain would cool the animosities that divided the valley. Thinking of Kate Roark, he doubted it. The clash had gone too far, feelings cut too deep. No rain would wash away the graves already dug.

Walden handed him his gun. "Won't do you much good," he said. "Sheriff collects all the hardware in town. Only way he can keep the whole place from goin' up in smoke."

Blaine holstered his Colt, accepting the information without comment.

At the edge of town a barricade had been set up. A deputy pushed himself out of the shade to stand beside the pole barrier as Blaine and the Rocking Chair crew drew near. "Collect your iron here, gents," he called out cheerfully.

"You settin' yourself up in business, Clemson?" one of the riders asked.

"I been thinkin' on it. How much you figger that old piece of yours would bring for scrap?"

"About the same as your horse, I reckon."

The mood was light enough, Blaine reflected. Apparently the sheriff's rule had been in effect long enough for the men to become used to it—perhaps even to accept its wisdom, for these hard-bitten men would prefer to choose the time and place of any fight. The real gunfighters among them took a cold and practical view of their trade. The cowmen were probably relieved to see the guns hung up. Few, if any, would back off from a challenge, but most punchers would be happier if the bloodletting didn't lead to a burial.

Reluctantly Blaine passed over his Colt, which was tagged and placed in a wooden tray with others like it. Clemson was a young man in his early twenties with a boyish face and round, innocent eyes, but he noted Blaine's unfamiliar name and gave him a quick, appraising glance.

Blaine frowned. Word would spread quickly in a town like this, and it would not go unnoticed that he had arrived in the company of the Rocking Chair bunch.

Had Kate Roark known as much when she sent along his escort?

He shrugged. There was nothing he could do about it now. A man who fretted over things he couldn't change had less time to give to those he could. Blaine's early years in Texas had taught him better, those years of parlaying a small stake and a lot of hard work into a working ranch. There were things you couldn't fight or howl against in that hostile land to any useful purpose—wind and rain, winter blizzard and summer heat, the crack of thunder that triggered a stampede or the flash flood that swept away a calf. If you didn't learn, if you railed against every perverse blow, the land chewed you up and spat you out, as empty as a husk.

And what Blaine hadn't learned then, he had been taught during these past two years of endless roaming, searching, chasing up blind canyons or trying to catch rumors as elusive and insubstantial as a dust devil. He had learned a stubborn patience.

Blaine left his buckskin at Anderson's Feed Barn, off to the left of the barricade at the southern edge of the town. A few of the other Rocking Chair hands did the same, while some rode ahead to tie their horses to the rail nearest their favorite saloon.

One of those who stopped at the barn was Clete Yeager. He confronted Blaine as he emerged from the stables.

The Rocking Chair foreman had ignored Blaine during the ride into town, just as the other hands, either taking their lead from Yeager or because they weren't sure of the newcomer themselves, had left him alone. But Blaine was not surprised now to find Yeager blocking his way. Sometimes hostility was natural and inevitable between two stubborn men. There was something between him and Yeager that hadn't been settled.

Blaine studied the gunman more closely than he had been able to before. Yeager was nearly half a head taller than Blaine, who was himself six feet in height. Long arms dropped from Yeager's squared-off shoulders. His dark face was triangular in shape, with the long chin marked by a cleft. His hair, thick eyebrows, and mustache were all black. He wore a soft cotton shirt, twill pants, expensive black boots and belt, the latter fastened with a heavy silver buckle. His gear was fancy for a ranch hand. Beside him Blaine looked gray and dusty and worn.

"I brought you in safe, Blaine," Yeager said, in a tone whose low pitch did not conceal its belligerence. "I did it because that's what Kate said." He used the woman's name with an easy familiarity, and Blaine wondered if he was intended to hear it that way. "That's as far as it goes. Keep out of my way from here on. Kate says you're some kind of a hunter, that you're huntin' a man. See to it your trackin' don't bring you back to the Rocking Chair."

"That all?" Blaine's voice was equally soft.

"No. Stay away from Kate Roark." As soon as the words were spoken, Blaine knew that this was the real message Yeager was delivering. He had sensed something in the exchanges between the owner of the Rocking Chair and her riding boss, a thread he couldn't follow for certain. But Yeager was telling him that Kate Roark was his woman, whether she admitted it yet or not. He was warning Blaine off.

Blaine wondered if Yeager had already asserted his claim. Somehow he doubted it. Her authority was too clear. Giving herself to Yeager as a woman would have weakened it, and Yeager could not have hidden the fact. His belligerence told an opposite story.

"I don't trust you and your story, Blaine. You talked your way around Kate, but I don't buy snake oil. If you stick in this valley at all, I'll take it to mean you're packin' lead for Simmons and his bunch, which is what I believe anyway. Remember that. Next time we meet, you won't catch me lookin' the other way."

"If I forget, you can remind me."

Blaine was aware of Walden standing nearby and taking this in. For another moment he and Yeager faced off. Then, without a word, Blaine stepped around the Rocking Chair's crew boss and walked away.

Yeager's low, contemptuous chuckle drifted after him. "That friend of yours is some kind of catamount, Walden," he said, loud enough for the words to carry. "I like the way he tucks in his tail."

"If that's what you think," Walden said, "you're makin' a long mistake."

Blaine did not look back.

* * *

He walked the gauntlet of the town's main street, ignoring the loungers on either side, until he came to the Viceroy Hotel, a two-story building with a brick front and clapboard sides at the north end of the street. A long porch spanned the front of the hotel, with a generous array of rocking chairs in place, two of them occupied by bent and grizzled old-timers who appeared not to notice the stranger arriving, although their desultory conversation ceased until he stepped into the lobby.

The interior was cool, wood-paneled, inviting after the dusty heat of the street. There was a bar adjoining the lobby on one side, a dining room on the other. Through the open doors of the latter Blaine saw white cloths on the tables and fresh flowers set into thin glass vases.

The young woman behind the counter watched him cross the lobby toward her. She had a pleasant, freckled face and a generous mouth that Blaine liked immediately. A crisp white shirtwaist set off her deeply tanned neck and throat attractively. He wondered how she managed to get so much sun while working in a hotel. She looked as if she belonged in the open, her blond hair set loose instead of coiled behind her head, her wide mouth laughing into the wind.

Her manner was carefully businesslike and without warmth. She offered Blaine his choice of a front room overlooking the street or a variety of lower-priced rooms at the back and sides of the building, facing adjoining structures or the alley. Signing the register, Blaine expressed surprise at the choice. "I thought you might be near full up, from the number of people in town."

Her answer was cool. "Most of those men won't pay for a hotel room, Mr. Blaine. And we get few travelers in Rush City these days. Not many care to come where there's trouble, and fewer stay." Her eyes seemed to question his presence in the hotel, and Blaine realized that she had quickly identified him with the narrow-eyed men he had seen along the boardwalks and in front of the town's saloons.

"Trouble will do that," he said.

"Yes." He caught her brief hesitation before she added, "This hotel is off limits for fighting. We don't want trouble here."

"That's fine," Blaine said soberly. "Should be a good place to get a night's rest."

Skepticism lingered in the young woman's eyes, but all she said was, "You'll find a bath at the end of the hall, if you'd care to use it."

Blaine grinned, catching the suggestion in her words. "Canyon could use a little water."

He trudged up the stairs, carrying his saddlebags over his shoulder. The room was plain but clean. It faced the blank wall of a weathered building next door. The stake he'd got from selling his ranch lands wouldn't run out for a while yet, but it was no longer so large that he could squander it for a room with a view. He wouldn't catch Ned Keatch from an upstairs window.

When he came downstairs an hour later, bathed and wearing his second shirt, which was polished thin but clean, the girl from the hotel desk was talking to a husky young man with curly blond hair and a white scar that stood out against the deep tan of his face. The two looked across the lobby at Blaine, and a prickly sensation made him think that they had been talking about him.

Blaine nodded pleasantly and went out. He wondered if, like the two graybeards on the porch, the pair in the lobby would take up their conversation where it had left off as soon as he was out of earshot.

The street was quiet. Unnaturally quiet. In any western town, even a dusty little place like this one, even in the high heat of an afternoon in August when a sensible man saved as much of his energy as he could, there was always noise, movement, stirrings of activity. Blaine missed the ring of a blacksmith's hammer, the jingle of spurs and the thud of boots along the boardwalk, the creak and rattle and dusty bouncing of a wagon, the movement of riders coming and going or of an occasional stage pulling in or out, the voices of women and children. For all the noise Blaine heard, Rush City might have been a ghost town.

Except that there were long shapes lounging in the shadows of the covered walk on the west side of the main street, which was now in deep shade, and half-hidden men holding up the doorways on the other side, back out of the sun. Blaine thought it didn't take much brainwork to figure that Rocking Chair hands were along the west side, which included the Palace saloon, while on the sunny side were those on the payrolls of the ranchers banded against Kate Roark's crew. It was a familiar story: one big spread that dominated a territory, with its owner making a lot of enemies while he became big, and a bunch of smaller outfits throwing together when trouble came to keep from being swallowed up.

Blaine spotted the sheriff's office across the way at the end of the block. He stepped down into the sun and crossed the street.

He felt a rising tension as he walked, listening only to the steady march of his own footsteps. The town was watching him, and waiting. For what?

He was nearing the Silver Bucket when a huge man shoved through the swinging doors of the saloon. He looked directly at Blaine, as if he had known he was coming, and stepped into his path on the elevated walk. He planted his legs wide and stood with his hands on his hips.

Blaine halted.

"I'm Walt Hamill," the big man said. "Work for Emlen Tucker and the Flying T. And you're in my way, stranger."

Blaine took in a slow, deep breath. So this was it.

He was aware of quick movements on both sides of the street. More men appeared on the boardwalks, faces peered from windows, late arrivals scurried and jostled for vantage points. It struck Blaine that everyone had known of the coming confrontation except him.

"There's room enough for two," he said quietly.

"Not here there ain't. You're on the wrong side of the street, mister. You belong over there, over in the dark with those other night crawlers."

"I have business over this way."

"No, you don't. You're with Rocking Chair, and—"

"I'm not with any outfit," Blaine answered tersely. "I'm goin' my own way."

"You're a liar," Walt Hamill said. "You was seen to come to town with Yeager and the rest of them polecats. So you got only one choice, mister. Either you walk across where you belong on your own two feet, or I boot your tail all the way across."

The street was very still now. The whole town was watching, listening, waiting. It had been expecting trouble, waiting for it to come, wondering only which way it would fall.

Cullom Blaine did not seek trouble with strangers. He had walked around Clete Yeager a short while back, but he was getting tired of being pushed. It had to stop here, or he wouldn't be able to leave his hotel room without being accosted.

Measuring Walt Hamill, he felt something like a chill at the back of his neck, a tingling of surprise. Hamill was so big that his head, although of normal size, was too small for his body, giving him a pinheaded appearance. His legs were like respectable-sized tree trunks, and his arms could have been planted for fence posts or laid out for railroad ties. He weighed well over two hundred pounds, and there wasn't a visible ounce any softer than an anvil. The sunny-side outfits had chosen their champion well, Blaine thought. And Hamill was a cowhand, not a gunfighter. His hands gave him away. They bore the thousand nicks and cuts and burns of any puncher. Blaine wondered if he bent horseshoes with them. He wouldn't worry about hurting them, the way a gunfighter would. And he'd jump into a rough-and-tumble like a boy into a swimming hole.

"Seems like I have one other choice," Blaine said softly.

"What's that?"

"I'm not askin' for trouble with you, Mr. Hamill. But if you don't get out of my way, I'm gonna cut you down so short you'll be able to run off to the circus as a midget."

With a joyous whoop, Walt Hamill charged.

Blaine ducked under the ponderous sweep of Hamill's arm and hammered his fist into the big man's belly. It was like hitting a two-inch-thick plank. He spun away from the next lunge, and the movement carried him off the boardwalk into the street.

A watcher yipped. "Get him now, Walt! Pulverize him!"

The yelling grew louder from both sides of the street as the fight went on, but Cullom Blaine scarcely heard it. Hamill was clumsy and slow, and Blaine avoided most of his wild swings, stepping inside frequently to land short, solid punches of his own. He knew they should have hurt, and once or twice Walt Hamill grunted and stopped for a second, but that was all. He just kept coming.

And it was impossible to avoid every blow. Blaine took one on the meat of his shoulder, and for the rest of the fight his left arm and shoulder were numb. Another grazed his head and left his ears ringing. The steady battering he took on his arms and sides, warding off the blows, slowly turned his arms to leaden weights.

At last Hamill caught him ducking. He grabbed Blaine with one bear's paw and held him long enough to deliver a crippling punch into his ribs. Unable to breathe, Blaine fell into Hamill, and the two men tumbled to the dust of the street.

Hamill locked both arms around Blaine and began to squeeze his spine. This close, Blaine caught the full smell of

the big man's breath, which could have been poured
directly from a jug. Blaine wondered if they simply filled
him with whiskey each day and sent him out to make kindling of the nearest Rocking Chair victim.

Then two things happened to make the fight personal and
unleash Blaine's anger. Hamill tried to cripple him with a
knee driving at his groin, and he bit Blaine's ear. Blaine took
most of the force of the kick on his thigh. He felt excruciat-
ing pain as Hamill's teeth tore at the lobe of his ear. The
agony goaded him to a whiplashing twist of his body that
broke Walt Hamill's hold. He rolled free.

Blaine wasn't breathing well, and the street danced before his eyes. His hands hurt and his arms were heavy, almost too heavy to lift. He knew the fight had to end
quickly.

He was first on his feet. When Hamill tried to rise, Blaine
met him with a knee flush on the jaw. The big man went
sprawling. He rose more slowly on the next try, blinking and
shaking his head as he reached his knees. Blaine locked his
hands together and brought them down like the blow of an
ax across the back of Hamill's neck. The huge cowboy ate
dust.

There were no words between them, and most of the
yelling on both sides of the street had ceased. The raw heaving of the two fighters' chests as they gulped air made almost the only sound.

Blaine waited for what seemed a long time before Walt
Hamill groped his way to his feet again, pawing air blindly.
"Over here, Shorty," Blaine taunted him.

Hamill charged at the sound of his voice. Blaine quickly
stepped aside, caught the big man's arm as he bulled past,
and swung him in a full cartwheel. At the end of the swing
Blaine released him, timing the release so that Hamill's
momentum rammed him head-on into a boardwalk pillar.

The whole boardwalk, supporting beams and pitched
roof and all, shivered.

Walt Hamill dropped flat on his face.

Blaine stood over him, heaving and shaking and dripping blood, unable to believe that Hamill wouldn't get up again, and keep getting up until Blaine could no longer find the strength even to lift his arms. But it didn't happen.

He heard a sharp, solid click behind him, then another. When he swung around he found a burly man in the street ten feet away, holding a shotgun level. Both locks on the double-barreled gun were pulled back to full cock. There was a star pinned to the stocky man's vest.

"All right, that's the end of it. You've had your fun, and you're both under arrest."

Blaine heard a scuffling sound. Hairs rose at the back of his neck as he spun around. Walt Hamill was stirring, trying to rise. His boots pushed feebly at the ground.

The sheriff glared at two men nearby on the boardwalk in front of the Silver Bucket. "You, Green! And, Swenson. Pick him up and bring him along." His scowling gaze swung back to Blaine. "If you can stand, you can walk. The jail's straight ahead. And I couldn't miss with this two-shoot gun at this distance even if I tried. What's your name, anyway?"

"Blaine," he mumbled through thick lips.

"All right, Mr. Blaine. Welcome to Rush City. Now move!"

FOUR

It was dusk when the sheriff unlocked the cell door. He left it open while he stepped inside and handed Blaine a tin plate of beans swimming in pork fat. "Reckon you can chew on that without hurtin' your teeth too much," he said.

Blaine looked skeptically at the plate. He was hungry, but he didn't know if he was *that* hungry. He understood why Clemson, the young deputy, had gone elsewhere for his evening meal.

In another cell, removed from Blaine's by an empty one, Walt Hamill sat up, blinking. He stared at Blaine and the sheriff from his cot. His face was battered and swollen, but he seemed calm. His eyes were more dull and baffled than angry, Blaine thought, as if he still hadn't figured out what happened.

"I'm Toland," the lawman said. "Sheriff here."

"Guessed as much." Blaine nodded toward the long-barreled shotgun stacked in a corner at the entrance to the cell block. "That's some kind of blunderbuss you carry."

Humor flickered in Toland's eyes. "It's been known to discourage more than one he-demon wearin' one of them peashooters you like to carry."

"Hey!" Walt Hamill interrupted. "What about me?"

"You'll get fed," Toland assured him.

Hamill peered along the cell block toward Blaine, who was tentatively sampling the beans. "That wasn't hardly a fair fight," he grumbled.

Blaine looked at him. "It stopped bein' that when you started biting."

Hamill studied him, as if he were weighing this. Suddenly he grinned. "Looks like I chewed off a piece."

"Pray it don't poison you," Blaine said. He felt no anger toward the big Flying-T cowboy now, and apparently Hamill felt none. At another time, in another place, it might all have been in fun, Blaine thought. But the ugly mood that pervaded this valley would not go away so easily.

He turned to Sheriff Toland. "What am I arrested for, Sheriff?"

"You're not," Toland answered. "I was just gettin' the two of you off the street to let things kind of cool off and settle down. You're free to go whenever you're ready."

Blaine eyed him speculatively. Toland had been around long enough to have seen his share of scrapes. Pushing forty or so in years, with a good portion of pink scalp showing through a thinning trace of hair, he had acquired the habit of letting the waistband of his pants ride under the swell of his belly. Blaine was not deceived. Toland had handled his shotgun with a cool authority, sealing an end to the fight and cutting off further trouble.

The sheriff returned to his front office, leaving the cell door and the connecting corridor door ajar. Blaine methodically finished off his plate of beans, vaguely surprised that he could still chew and swallow. His hands were raw and puffy, the bitten ear still throbbed, and when he even attempted to change position his ribs ached. Otherwise, he thought wryly, he was as shiny as a new dollar.

Toland was behind his desk, tilting back in a wooden swivel chair, when Blaine emerged. He made no comment, but his eyes weren't lazy.

"You could have stopped that fight sooner," Blaine said thoughtfully.

"I could have," the sheriff admitted. "But I'll tell you somethin', Mr. Blaine. We get maybe one or two fights like that every day. I collect the guns as well as I can, but I don't find all the knives and I can't do anything about a man's fists

or his temper. But it seems like a good fight lets off some of
the steam for a while." He paused. "You can go, Blaine. I
doubt you'll have any more trouble tonight, but you'd best
stay on your own side of the street all the same."

"Which side is that, Sheriff?"

"You know as well as I do." Toland scowled. He didn't
like evasions. "You rode in with the Rocking Chair
bunch."

From his cell in back, Walt Hamill called out in complaint. "Hey, what about me? Sheriff?"

"You'll get out after he's gone," Toland told him. He
smiled thinly at Blaine. "No use temptin' fate."

Blaine laughed. "You'll get no argument from me there,
Sheriff." He made no move to leave. Toland seemed a reasonable man for a peace officer. There were some questions
he could answer if he wanted to. "Seems like everyone's
hell-bent to sign me up with the Rocking Chair," he said.
"You've all got it wrong."

The sheriff eyed him quizzically, waiting.

"They jumped me last night on the trail, up near what
they called the south pass. Kate Roark sent along some of
her crew to see me into town. To make sure I didn't stay on
Rocking Chair land, I reckon."

"You're a fortunate man, Mr. Blaine." Toland showed his
surprise. "Kate isn't always so generous."

Blaine let that pass. "I didn't come here to sign up with
anyone." He paused, weighing the wisdom of announcing
his purpose. "I'm lookin' for a man."

Toland's boots hit the floor. "Bounty hunter?" he
snapped. "If that's it, I'll find your hide hangin' on a fence,
Blaine. There's too many hard-cases in this valley—"

"No," Blaine interrupted patiently. "I'm not interested in
any reward. It's personal."

The lawman studied him for a moment with new interest.
He had put Blaine down as just another gun for hire, the lat-
est in a parade that boded ill for the peaceableness of the

town and the whole valley. But there was something different about him. He was hard, dangerous. Toland had witnessed or heard of at least a score of fights involving Walt Hamill, but he'd never heard of big Walt being put down before. Any man who could do that with his fists and his feet was dangerous. But this Blaine, Toland realized, lacked something the lawman had come to recognize by instinct in a real gunsmoker. He was cold enough. His eyes, green-flecked and steady, yielded nothing. But something was missing. An arrogance, perhaps. The pride of a man who lived by the swiftness of his gun hand. A bloodless quality.

"Why should I be interested in helpin' you find this man?" Toland asked, probing.

"He's wanted by the law down Texas way, if that's reason enough."

"But no reward?"

"You're welcome to it," Blaine answered curtly. "Like I said, it's personal."

Toland opened a drawer and pulled out a sheaf of posters. In a second drawer he found another pile. When he put them together, they made a stack six inches high. "You see them dodgers, Blaine? Every one of 'em is for a wanted man. Sometimes two or three on one list. I don't even have time to read 'em all. If I did, I suppose there's a hell of a good chance I could find a dozen men or more in this valley answering those descriptions. If I tried it, I wouldn't have time for nothin' else, and whilst I was at it this town would go to hell in a hurry."

"The one I'm lookin' for, his name is Ned Keatch."

Toland slowly shook his head. "I can't help you. Never heard the name, leastwise not that I can recall. Anyways, you sound like trouble to me, Blaine. Trouble I don't need. I don't care what you want this Keatch for, there'll be no gunplay in this town while I'm sheriff. And any man starts a shooting war anywhere in this valley will answer to the law.

I'm sittin' on a case of dynamite, Blaine. I won't just sit there whilst somebody lights the fuse under me. That plain enough?"

"You don't exactly waltz around the pole, Sheriff." Blaine turned away, thinking that he had learned all that he would here. But at the doorway something nudged his memory and he swung back. "I'd like to talk to this man Simmons. Would that be against the law?"

"It might not be the smartest idea you ever had," Toland said. "Not after today."

"Might be I could set that straight." Blaine smiled thinly. "Save you the trouble of breakin' up another head-knocking."

"Simmons is in town," Toland said grudgingly. "He heads up the Cattlemen's Association. That's what they call themselves. Just about every rancher in the valley is a member, 'ceptin' Kate Roark." He hesitated. "It was Sean Roark pushed 'em into it, damn him. Got himself killed for his trouble."

"Who shot him, Sheriff?"

"Any special reason you want to know?"

"No. But it might explain some things."

Toland chewed his lower lip, speculating. "Man by the name of Collins done it. Quick trigger no-account the Association hired. Simmons knows he was responsible, but by the time he learned his lesson it was too late."

"What happened to Collins?"

"He lit a shuck soon as it happened, but I never got a chance to put out one of these reward dodgers on him." The lawman slapped the stack on his desk with a pudgy hand. "He didn't run fast enough to get away from the Rocking Chair bunch. When they found the old man on the trail where he was gunned down—"

"Bushwhacked?" Blaine broke in. "I heard Roark was killed in a shootout. I figgered it must've been a town fight."

Toland shook his head. "Roark was too smart to be caught that way. They wore guns here in town then—that was before I started collectin' 'em—but he wouldn't have let himself be slickered into a street fight with some gunfighter. No, he was on Rocking Chair land when it happened, headin' back that way from town. He was alone, and he'd have been careful of an ambush, not havin' anyone to back him up. Seems like what he didn't expect was to have one of those Association killers ride right up to him on his own land, look him straight in the eye, and draw iron." Seemingly tired of chewing his lip, the lawman fished in a vest pocket until he found a wooden match, which he stuck between his teeth and talked around. "That was one thing I could never figger, Roark lettin' himself be jumped alone like that."

"If he was alone, how do you know Collins killed him?"

Toland gave Blaine a withering stare. "You think I don't have the brains to ask myself that? He did it, all right. His own people, the ones who hired him, were responsible. Reason Collins met Roark where he did is 'cause he was sent." The sheriff scowled with recollected outrage. "The way Simmons and the Association people tell it, all they wanted was to palaver. Roark wasn't talkin' to Simmons by then, so Collins was picked to meet the old man and set up a general confab." Toland paused. "It *could* have been that way, I'm not sayin' it wasn't, but you can't get Kate Roark to believe it. And anyway it was a damned fool thing to do. Simmons should've known better than to pick the man he did. Collins met Roark like he was supposed to, but they must've had words when they come together, and Collins cut him down."

"What happened then?"

"He ran, of course," Toland said disgustedly. "The Rocking Chair crew made up their own posse and chased him down. Took 'em a day and a half, but they run him to ground."

"Was Yeager with that posse?"

"He was."

"If I was to take a guess," Blaine said thoughtfully, "on who it was that put Collins under when they caught up to him, I'd name Yeager."

The sheriff cocked an eyebrow at him. "That don't take much of a soothsayer, but do you mind tellin' me why?"

Blaine was silent. His hunch about Yeager was predicated on the gunman's present position with the Rocking Chair. Kate Roark would have been grateful to the man who put her father's killer in the ground, and she would have been looking for a strong man to carry on the fight. And Clete Yeager would have been eager to prove himself the right choice.

He said, "Just a hunch."

"If you're wonderin' why he's still ridin' loose," the sheriff said, "that home-grown posse was out of my county by the time they caught Collins. And even if they hadn't been, there wasn't much I could've done. Way most folks see it, shootin' Collins don't half make up for Roark's killing. Range wars make their own law, Blaine. I can keep the damper on here in town, but in the rest of this valley. . . ." He shrugged. "I'm one man. My deputy's a good 'un, but he's still green. Maybe if the Rocking Chair bunch and the Association kill enough of each other off, we'll be able to stop the ones that's left from feudin'." Toland leaned forward, his gaze bleak, as if he had become used to expecting the worst of human nature. "Collins is gone, but that don't stop what he started. That's why I don't want another grudge killing in this valley, Blaine. If you find your man and do what you want, you'll figger that's the end of it. You'll just ride out, if we don't bury you. And you'll leave more trouble behind, the way Collins did. Leave me with a shootin' war. If Collins hadn't put Sean Roark belly up, like as not things wouldn't have got out of hand the way they have. Roark was a bull-headed son, but you could reason with him sometimes after he cooled off. He could keep a halter on the likes of Yeager, and Brad Simmons was like a son to him once. But after what happened, you can't talk to Kate." He brooded momentarily over this reflection. "She went wild when Sean was killed. I think a woman hates harder than a man, Blaine."

Blaine did not answer. He thought of the proud young woman who had given him breakfast that morning and offered him a job. It was easier now to see what lay behind her bitterness.

"Thanks for the information, Sheriff," he said. Then he added, "I still want to talk to Simmons. How might I find him?"

He wasn't sure that Toland was going to reply, but after a moment the burly sheriff said grudgingly, "You can ask over at the hotel. Likely he's there, and if he isn't you can talk to Nancy Cronin at the registration desk. She can point him out, or say where he is, if she's a mind to."

Blaine had a sudden recollection. "Would he be a lanky kind of gent, curly blond hair, and a white scar across one cheek?"

Toland raised an eyebrow. "That's him."

Blaine nodded, turning toward the door. "Thanks again."

Toland's voice stopped him in the doorway. "There's somethin' else you ought to know, Blaine." When Blaine looked back the lawman rose. He leaned a meaty hip against the side of his desk and tugged at his sagging pants fruitlessly, more as a gesture than anything else. "It was Kate Roark give him that scar. With her whip. You see, Kate and Simmons was engaged to be married before the real trouble started. Maybe that's partly why she went so crazy when her daddy was gunned down by one of the Association's hired guns. So you see, Mr. Blaine, you stepped into a real hornet's nest for sure. Don't stir it up any more."

Blaine stared at him for a moment in surprise at this unexpected revelation. Then he stepped through the doorway into the closing dusk.

The street was quiet—even more ominously quiet than before. Now the walks and the alleys between buildings were in shadow, and Blaine had the feeling of being watched by a hundred eyes. Thoughtfully, an ironic smile touching his lips, he stepped out into the empty street. The message was there for anyone who cared to read it as he walked on steadily, his boots kicking up a trail of dust to mark his path, making a center line between the opposing sides, choosing neither.

He reached the hotel without incident.

The lobby was quiet. A man in a black eastern-style suit was eating alone in the dining room. He looked across the room at Blaine hopefully, but Blaine turned aside.

The young woman was not at the desk.

Briefly Blaine lingered in the lobby. Simmons was obviously not there, and Nancy Cronin was nowhere around. Peeking in at the kitchen, he found a Chinese cook at work along with a watery-eyed, worn-out codger who was washing dishes.

Frowning, Blaine went slowly up the stairs.

His room was dark. He was inside before he felt the skin-crawling sensation of warning.

A hammer clicked, and a voice said softly, "Come in, Mr. Blaine. And close the door."

Blaine stood motionless. His right hand had gone instinctively to his hip, and found it bare.

FIVE

A match flared. Cullom Blaine squinted against the sudden brightness. The man sitting in the room's only chair touched the flame to a lamp. Otherwise his hands were empty. The gun whose hammer Blaine had heard was held by another intruder, a lean and hungry-looking man on the other side of the bed. The gun's muzzle did not waver from Blaine's middle.

"Wait outside in the hall, McEwan," Brad Simmons said. "Mr. Blaine and I have some talking to do."

McEwan checked a protest, shrugged, and edged carefully past Blaine to the door. Simmons waited until the door had closed. "I'm not looking for a fight with you, Mr. Blaine," he said with an engaging grin. "Not after seeing you tangle with Walt Hamill."

Blaine was silent a moment, letting his quick anger subside. Simmons had a high-handed way of getting to see him for a talk. "You could have waited downstairs for me," he said.

Simmons nodded. "If I knew where you stood, that's what I would have done. But I don't know. That's what I'm here to find out."

"With a gun cocked."

"I don't like that part of it any more than you do. But these aren't normal times in Rush City, Mr. Blaine. And I don't know who you are."

"This isn't the way to find out." But Blaine's anger had cooled enough for him to wonder if Simmons might have had a sensible reason for this reception. If he had expected to confront a gunman on the Rocking Chair's payroll, this way of meeting might have seemed a prudent precaution. "I thought the sheriff was collecting all the guns in town."

Simmons spread out both hands, palms up. "Toland and his deputy can't search every saddlebag and pocket. It's really a kind of honor system, Mr. Blaine. Thing of it is, any man who *uses* a gun in town knows he'll answer for it. I don't propose to have Mr. McEwan use that six-holer." He paused. "Not unless you're a troublemaker, and there's no other way for us to reason together."

Cullom Blaine felt heat at the back of his neck. "Mr. Simmons—I take it that's your name—I'm gettin' a little tired of having people shove guns in my face or shake a fist under my nose, and then tell me how much trouble I'm causing. If you don't want trouble, and you want to talk, send your man away. Otherwise we have nothin' to talk about." He paused a moment before adding softly, "And the next man points a gun at me better be prepared to use it."

Brad Simmons' eyes narrowed. He stared speculatively at Blaine for a long moment. Then he rose, tall in the narrow room, and went to the door. He spoke briefly to the man in the hall, and Blaine then heard the clump of the lean gunman's boots going down the stairs.

"All right, Mr. Blaine," Simmons said as he returned to the room, "let's put some cards face up."

"I'll play you one," Blaine said. "Face card with a man's name on it. Name of Ned Keatch."

Simmons frowned. "I don't know the name. What makes you think I would?"

"He's wanted for murder and robbery. He's a gunfighter, Mr. Simmons, and from what I hear tell you've been interviewin' men like him."

Simmons flushed. "You make it sound like I started all this."

"Didn't you?"

"No!"

"I was told you hired the man gunned down Sean Roark of the Rocking Chair—and you sent that man to meet Roark. Are you sayin' I heard wrong?"

Simmons flinched visibly, and the flush of color drained from his face. The accusation had hit home, and it took some of the self-assurance out of the young man. Stiffly he said, "I'll admit I'm responsible for that, and it's not a soft pillow to sleep on. But I never wanted it to happen. My fault was not in hiring Collins—that was the man's name— but in not riding close enough herd on him. He seemed . . . well, I didn't think he'd lose his head the way he did. I should have been more careful, and if I had Roark would be alive today. But the trouble would be the same," he went on with an insistence that sounded defensive. "Collins wasn't the first gunfighter to be hired on either side. Trouble's been comin' to this valley for a long time, Mr. Blaine, and it was mostly Sean Roark's doing."

"I heard you was friends once."

There was fleeting surprise in Simmons' eyes, as if he wondered where Blaine had heard so much. "We were. Kate Roark and I . . . hell, I've known them since I was a boy. Sean taught me most of what I know about raisin' cattle. I liked him, admired him—he was like a father to me, Mr. Blaine. I never knew my own. Trouble was, I grew up eventually. And I began to see that some of the things I'd admired weren't really so admirable."

Scowling now, Simmons prowled the room, head down as if he were counting the planks of the floor. He stopped at the window to stare out. There was nothing he could see there, Blaine thought. Opposite the window was a blank wall, and the darkness made the canyon between buildings pitch black. But Simmons had obviously turned up a painful and troubled memory. He wouldn't have seen anything else if the sun had been shining.

"Sean Roark thought he owned this valley, Mr. Blaine. He was here first, and he had it all his own way for a long time.

Give him credit, he showed us all that cattle could be raised
in this part of the country, and sold at a profit. When others
began to want a piece of the pie, Sean felt like they were
stealing from him. He grudged every blade of grass another
man's cattle ate, or every drop of water drunk by anything
but a critter with the Rocking Chair burned into its hide.
But you can't stop other people from wanting a share, Mr.
Blaine. There's no way one man could keep an open range
like this all to himself. Roark tried. He rode roughshod over
anyone who got in his way. He accused some of his neighbors of rustling cattle or stealing horses—I think he half
believed it in the end, he said it so often. He'd fence off
water if he thought he needed it for his own, even if it
meant another man's cattle died of thirst. He scared some of
the small ranchers out, and bought up others' paper at the
bank to squeeze them out. But he couldn't make us all quit.
That's why this fight had to come, whether Sean lived or
died."

Simmons swung around to stare at Blaine. There was a
harshness in his expression, but his eyes remained defensive,
as if he needed to justify his words to this stranger, or to
himself.

"I reckon this drought helped to bring it to a head,"
Blaine suggested. "This valley's dried up."

Simmons nodded soberly. "Seems like we haven't had
rain enough to fill a bucket these past two summers, and not
much snow last winter. All the water's low, and some of the
creeks are plumb dry. Hell, I had a lake on my place that's
down to a muddy bottom now. It's got to end sometime, but
. . . I doubt it will make any difference. Not the way Kate
Roark feels. She's hired herself as many guns as the Association has, Mr. Blaine, maybe more. Worst of the lot is the
man you rode into town with—Clete Yeager. I can't prove
what I say, but one of our people was burned out this
spring, Art Cronin—his daughter works here at the hotel, on

the desk most days—and Cronin was caught in that fire. I think Yeager set that fire, him or his men."

Cullom Blaine felt a chill that threatened to crawl down his spine. He blocked it off, stilling the harrowing memory it awakened.

There was a silence. Brad Simmons fumbled in his pockets until he found the makings of a cigarette. "Smoke, Mr. Blaine?" When Blaine shook his head, Simmons proceeded to build a cigarette and light it. The action gave him time to sort out his thoughts and feelings, Blaine thought. Perhaps he felt that he had talked too much.

"I don't know why I've told you all this," Simmons said, confirming Blaine's hunch.

"I asked you about Ned Keatch."

"Yes. . . . Well, I never heard of him." A speculation caused him to look at Blaine sharply. "What do you want with him? You're not wearing a badge."

"That's my business."

"If he's working for the Association, that makes it mine," Simmons answered.

"No," Blaine said in a very quiet tone. "If I find Keatch, it has nothin' to do with you or the Association or Kate Roark."

Simmons checked a retort as he stared at Blaine. In that moment he saw something in this quiet man he had not glimpsed clearly before. It was something anyone who had known the harsh life of the frontier, and the men it forged, could recognize when they saw it. It made Simmons momentarily uneasy, less sure of himself. Who was this man? What did he want? What kind of fire burned so deep inside him?

He thought of the fight he had witnessed between this man and big Walt Hamill. There had been a moment there, near the end, when some kind of simmering fury seemed to explode in Blaine. And he had stomped Walt like he was whipping a boy. And picked him up like it was nothing at all, and threw him. . . .

Simmons scowled. He was just a man. His boots pinched like any other man's. "Are you saying you're not working for the Rocking Chair?" he demanded.

"You didn't have to hide in my room to learn that."

Simmons colored slightly again, but, without being able to say exactly why—or not willing to—he refrained from any belligerent retort. Instead he asked quietly, "Then how come you tangled with Walt Hamill?"

"It was his idea," Blaine answered tersely.

Simmons studied him, taking this in. Then he looked away from Blaine's unblinking gaze. Packed too loosely, his cigarette had burned short quickly, and he searched for a place to stub it out. Finding nothing else, he dropped it onto a dish on top of the oak bureau opposite the bed.

When he looked up, he appeared to have come to a decision. "All right, Mr. Blaine. I was wrong about you, and I apologize. I hope you'll understand . . . we have to know where a man stands."

"Now you know."

"Yes. . . ." Simmons turned toward the door. He hesitated with his hand on the doorknob, then swung back. "That doesn't mean that—"

"Let me ask a question, Mr. Simmons," Blaine cut him off. "What would you have proposed to do if you found out I was workin' for Kate Roark?"

Simmons drew himself up. He was a tall man, but he was neither as big nor as certain of himself as he tried to appear. He would have a rough time if it came to a real showdown with Kate Roark, Blaine decided. She had something on her side that Simmons lacked. His anger and self-righteousness, and that of the other ranchers, would burn out long before her hate.

"I'd have tried to buy you off," Simmons said with a

frankness that carried conviction. "It's been done before. And if that hadn't worked, I'd have tried to scare you off."

"Has that been done before, too?"

"It has," Simmons answered stiffly, with a trace of pride. "We're not helpless, Mr. Blaine. There's good men on our side. Men who won't give up this fight. That's something Kate hasn't learned." He hesitated before he added, "It's something you'd best understand as well. There's no way you can go up against one of the Association's men alone and make it stick. I don't know your Ned Keatch, but you'll do well to look for him elsewhere. Don't stick your nose into our fight."

This took some courage to say, in the face of the lingering uneasiness this quiet-spoken stranger had awakened in Simmons. The relief that he had found the spine to say it showed in Simmons' eyes, and Blaine marked it there. He was young, Blaine thought. Maybe there was more to him than he had discovered yet himself. Evidently he had won the respect of his neighbors, the other small ranchers in the valley, if he was their elected leader and spokesman. Evidently, too, women liked his lanky, ambling good looks and winning manner. He had been engaged to Kate Roark at one time. And there had been a sense of intimacy in the way Nancy Cronin spoke to him in the lobby of the hotel earlier in the day, as Blaine was passing through.

Blaine dismissed the tug of sympathy, the knowledge that he could have liked this young man at another time and place. "Be glad you didn't have to try to scare me off, Mr. Simmons," he said with a wintry smile. "It would've taken more than McEwan's gun."

"More than the Cattlemen's Association?" Simmons retorted.

"I have no grievance with your Association. Not unless you're hidin' Ned Keatch behind your flag. But I'll tell you this, Mr. Simmons. If I found a rattlesnake in my bed, I wouldn't just roll over and go to sleep with him. I'd throw him out. That's what Keatch is, and if he's here in this valley, I'll find him. Don't let me find him in your bed."

As he finished talking Blaine unexpectedly took a firm, deliberate stride toward the door, forcing Simmons either to stand his ground or retreat. The young man backed off. Before he knew how it happened he found himself in the hall, hearing Blaine's crisp "Good night!" and watching the door close.

Simmons stood staring at the door, feeling a cold weight in the pit of his stomach that he didn't like at all.

* * *

When Nancy Cronin saw Simmons coming down the stairs, she slipped into Henry Allison's office. She had been there when the man called Cullom Blaine returned to the hotel, choosing to stay out of sight because she had never been very good at dissembling—and Blaine had a pair of very penetrating eyes that gave her the notion he could look right into her mind.

Waiting in Allison's office, she wondered what had happened upstairs. It couldn't have been troublesome, she thought, or Brad would not have sent McEwan downstairs.

The office was empty, a safe place to talk. Henry Allison, the owner of the hotel, was away in Cheyenne on business, not due back for another two days. Nancy, in the meanwhile, was more or less in charge of the hotel, although Mrs. Allison came in to help out on the desk and to fuss over the help, generally providing more commotion than assistance.

The office was safe, too, for her to be alone with Brad Simmons. The thought of him coming to her room, as he had suggested, brought a flutter to her stomach. She hated this knowledge. When would she get over it? Never? Any chance that Simmons would ever see her as anything but an ally in his fight had vanished long ago. Kate Roark had seen to that.

Simmons knocked lightly and stepped into the office. She experienced a quick, breathless feeling when he approached her. "Thanks, Nancy," he said, with a nonchalant grin that did not help her nervous stomach at all. "You can relax now. No trouble. No blood spilt on Allison's sheets and curtains."

"Don't say such things," she said quickly. "If I'd thought for a minute—"

"I know. Anyway, it's over." He frowned. "For now."

"How did it go?"

Simmons shook his head. There was something baffled in his eyes. "I'm not sure. He's a strange man, Nancy, not at all what I expected. But at least he's not working for the Rocking Chair."

She felt relief. The possibility that she might have been instrumental in bringing Simmons to a dangerous confrontation with one of Kate Roark's hired gunmen had been a weight in her chest for the past hour, like something eaten that refused to go down.

Simmons kicked a chair around with one boot—she thought instantly of Henry Allison's dismay at such careless treatment of his furniture, but she said nothing—and looped a leg across the chair, straddling it backward with his hands on the ladder back. Nancy retreated to another chair, thinking that he did everything with a careless grace.

She listened intently while Simmons recounted his conversation with Blaine. When he had finished she asked, "Do you think he'll take your warning?"

Simmons slowly shook his head, his brown eyes sober. They were the nicest eyes, she thought. They—

She looked away, thinking again how poor she was at hiding her thoughts, how quick to give herself away.

But Simmons hadn't noticed. "No," he said. "I don't think so. Whatever he's after . . . I tell you, Nancy, I wouldn't want to be in this Ned Keatch's boots! This Blaine . . . he's like some big rock rolling down a hill. If Keatch was at the bottom, Blaine would just roll right over anything or anyone in his way. He—" Simmons broke off, smiling ruefully. "Listen to me talk. It isn't as if Blaine is just pawing around for turmoil anywhere he can find it. He's after only one thing."

"But if Keatch isn't here—"

"We don't know that. He could be, maybe going by another handle. Blaine must have some reason to think he is."

"What will you do, Brad?"

"I don't know." Simmons lifted his shoulders and dropped them with a heavy sigh, as if the weight of the world were on them. Which, in a way, it was, Nancy thought sympathetically, wishing the other ranchers hadn't burdened him with so much responsibility by electing him as their leader. She had felt a strong pride, however, when she had heard the news. Brad Simmons was younger than most of the others. His selection was a mark of the respect they had for him. "We'll talk it over at our next meeting. Thing is, if Keatch is working for someone in the Association . . ." He shook his head, worry showing plainly for the first time.

Abruptly he rose, swinging the chair around carelessly and dropping it near where he had found it. Nancy Cronin also rose automatically, facing him with her hands folded before her, not quite sure what to do with them, like one time when she had had to recite a poem in front of her class at school.

"We'll work it out," Simmons said. "At least now we know where we stand as far as Blaine is concerned. Thanks to you."

He placed his hands over her shoulders and looked down at her, his mouth and his eyes smiling. She felt as if she could neither move nor breathe. All she could do was wait helplessly.

"We wouldn't have been able to pull this meeting off if Allison had been here. I know how he wants to keep this hotel off limits for trouble, so neither side can claim it. But there's no reason he has to know."

"It's . . . all right, Brad. It's over now."

"Yes." He regarded her quizzically. Then he leaned forward suddenly and planted a kiss on her forehead. "You're the best, Nancy Cronin. Your pa would be proud of you. I promise, we'll make it up to you for what was done to him."

He turned to leave. Nancy remained motionless, the print of his kiss burning on her forehead, managing only a faint smile as he glanced back at her and waved before he went out.

She stayed in Allison's office alone for several minutes, waiting to get her emotions under wraps. It was only when she finally felt ready to emerge that an errant thought crossed her mind, awakened by something Brad Simmons had said. And for one moment even Brad Simmons was banished from her mind, replaced by the stranger in the room upstairs, the man called Cullom Blaine.

SIX

Blaine was up early. He scraped off a week's growth of whiskers, thankful for the welcome change of hot water in the pan. When he came down to breakfast, he was surprised to find the dining room relatively crowded. Apparently the hostile factions found it convenient to accept the hotel as neutral ground.

He ate his second hearty breakfast in two days—thick sliced bacon, eggs, pan-fried potatoes, fresh bread, and coffee, thick and black. The occasions when a man on the prod could eat well, with plenty of hot food and a cloth on the table, were rare. Blaine took advantage of them when he could. He didn't know when he would eat his next good meal, or where.

A number of his fellow diners seemed particularly aware of him, evidenced in sidelong glances and studious avoidance of his eyes rather than in any show of welcome. By now, he thought, both of the valley's feuding parties had heard why he was here. The word would reach the ears of Ned Keatch soon enough, if it hadn't already.

Blaine had had brief glimpses of nearly a score of Kate Roark's riders. None of them resembled the man he had come to find. Keatch was almost certain to be careful of strangers, and he might well have stayed out of sight. It was equally possible that he had been hired by one of the other ranchers in the valley, members of the Cattlemen's Association. Those ranches would be scattered all over the area, in the valley and on the surrounding hills and benches. Keatch could be at any one of them.

Blaine's ready announcement of his name and his purpose had been calculated, in the hope of prodding Keatch into some kind of a reaction. A guilty man never rested easy. Blaine's hunch was that Keatch wouldn't be able to stand having a hunter breathing so close to the back of his neck. Not for long.

"May I join you for coffee, Mr. Blaine?"

Blaine scraped back his chair, clumsy in his surprise. Before he could rise Nancy Cronin had slipped into another chair. There was no visible signal, but an instant later the waitress appeared with a second cup and a pot of fresh coffee. Blaine settled back, studying the freckle-faced young woman he had met at the registration desk. "Sure enough, Miss Cronin. Glad to have company."

She gave a little laugh. "I doubt anyone else would dare sit with you. They're not sure enough of you, Mr. Blaine. People in Antelope Valley have become cautious about . . . strangers."

"But you're throwing caution to the winds."

"Not exactly."

"Is that because you've already talked to Brad Simmons, and you figure you know all about me?"

His bluntness disconcerted her a little, but she recovered quickly. "Does anyone know all about you, Mr. Blaine?" When he didn't answer the smile faded from her lips. Which was a pity, Blaine thought. She had a pleasant smile, and good eyes that caught the warmth of that smile. Blaine had heard it argued that you couldn't tell anything about another person, man or woman, just from looking into their eyes. He didn't believe it. Some eyes were open windows. Some shifted too much, refusing to let you see into them. Others were flat, opaque, like the eyes of some of the gunmen holding up the posts on either side of Rush City's main street, but even this was revealing. Eyes might be clouded by pain or drink or age, but they almost always told a story if your own vision was clear enough to read it. A card player might learn to mask his eyes as he ruled the muscles of his face, but he had to work hard at it. He had to be careful not only of what he revealed but also of where he looked. Not many were really good at it. A man who was generally had a tall stack of chips in front of him. And his success told you as much about him as did the flat eyes of the gunfighter.

"What is it, Mr. Blaine?"

"Beg pardon, ma'am?"

"You were staring at me so. I wondered . . . what you saw."

Blaine smiled, but his did not reach his eyes. "My apologies, Miss Cronin. I didn't mean to stare. But I'll have to admit you've surprised me."

"How?"

"You told Brad Simmons about me, gave him the key to my room, and stayed out of sight when I came back to the hotel. Yet this morning you're joining me for coffee."

The young woman's cheeks flamed, visible even beneath the healthy tan of her skin. Simmons' revelation explained that color, Blaine thought. She must have lived with her father on their ranch before they were burned out. She wasn't really a town woman.

"How . . . how can you be so sure of that?" she asked, faltering.

"Didn't you?"

She hesitated for only a few seconds. "Yes, I did, Mr. Blaine. I suppose you think that was quite wrong of me."

Blaine shrugged. He was not angry, she saw. It struck her that little things, trifles, would not disturb him. The impression renewed the resolution which had brought her to his table. She sipped at her coffee, searching for the right words to broach what was in her mind. Then she realized that with this man there was no need to tiptoe around it, and no point at all in dissembling.

"I did that because Brad Simmons is . . . my friend. He was also a good friend to my father. He's dead. He was—"

"Simmons told me," Blaine said gently.

Her eyes revealed surprise. But she had started now, and she hurried on before her determination would have a chance to waver. "Brad thought you might be another gunfighter, hired by the Rocking Chair. He tells me that's not so." She looked to him for confirmation, but his face was expressionless. He wasn't making it easy, she thought. "Then you know I own a ranch now—I'm the only family Pa had. We have—that is, I have a small herd of cattle, and some good horses. The land is good, Mr. Blaine. It's west of here. There's good water even now, almost the only good water left in that end of the valley. I think that's why they had to drive us out. The water, and the fact that the Paradise is right in the middle, in between Luke Hammond's place and the Flying T north of Paradise, and the Rocking Chair to the south."

"Paradise?" Blaine asked.

Nancy Cronin blinked, her eyes suddenly moist. "That's what Pa called it. That's what he thought it was. But it took Ma, and now it's taken him, so I guess it wasn't any paradise for them." She blinked again, but her chin lifted and her lips tightened. "I don't care, it's my land, Mr. Blaine, and I mean to hold it. I won't give it up. I won't be driven out."

More interested now, Blaine wondered what she was leading up to. "You were sayin' Paradise is right in the middle?"

"That's right. Kind of in between. The smaller spreads are mostly north and east of us, and Sean Roark claimed everything else around. As long as we were there, Kate Roark couldn't claim our grass and water for the Rocking Chair's cattle."

"Excuse me, Miss Cronin, but I take it what you're sayin' is, you believe Kate Roark is responsible for burning you out?"

"Why . . . of course! Brad must have told you that. No one else would do such a thing. Pa was a member of the Association, Mr. Blaine. They had no reason to turn against us."

Blaine nodded thoughtfully. What she said made sense, but he had learned that the obvious explanation was not always the true one. "Did anyone see who did it?"

"No," Nancy Cronin admitted. "It started at night. The barn went up first. Maybe they didn't even mean for the fire to spread to the house, but it did. It happened so fast, you wouldn't believe how fast it was. There were two men in the bunkhouse that night, but they didn't give a warning. One of them was found in the barn. Maybe he tried to put the fire out, and something fell on him. He was burned alive." She was speaking in a rush now, her eyes wide, looking beyond Blaine toward that awful night. "My bedroom was downstairs. I smelled the smoke and heard the fire, it was like a big wind howling. I was able to get out through a window. Pa slept upstairs, and he was a sound sleeper. I guess he never heard anything. He—" She broke off. "Mr. Blaine, what's wrong?"

"Nothing." His tone was flat, his eyes curiously bright and hard. "Go on, Miss Cronin."

"There isn't much more. Pa died in the fire. I wanted to stay on—I tried to—but no sooner would I hire a man than he'd be run off. Scared off, Mr. Blaine. It got so I couldn't hire anyone to work there, and I couldn't go it alone. Anyway, Brad—Mr. Simmons—didn't think it was safe for me to be there alone. I moved into town, and Mr. Allison gave me a room here at the hotel. I work for it," she added a little defensively.

There was silence for a while. Blaine noticed that the breakfast crowd had begun to thin out. He wondered how many of them had observed his conversation with Nancy Cronin with more than idle interest. Little would happen in Rush City that wasn't noted, he thought, and sifted for its importance.

"You said there were two men in that bunkhouse," he said. "What happened to the other man?"

"Sawyer? I don't know. He wasn't found in the bunkhouse or the barn, and no one's ever seen him again. I suppose he was run off, or just lit out when he saw what was happening."

"More'n likely," Blaine murmured.

The young woman stared at him, trying to read his reaction, wondering what it was she had briefly glimpsed in his eyes. But that odd brightness was gone now, and his face was once again expressionless. A hard face, she thought, almost cruel. He was not a man who would be easily frightened. Kate Roark, she was quite certain, would have tried to hire him. He must have turned her down. He hadn't been intimidated by Walt Hamill or Clete Yeager or Brad Simmons. He was the man she needed.

"Mr. Blaine," she said firmly, "I'd like to hire you."

Blaine did not answer immediately. If the offer surprised him, she could not tell it. He continued to regard her with a steady, probing gaze that made her feel exposed and vulnerable. Well, she had nothing to hide. The reason she had given him was an honest one. But as she waited nervously, she began to wonder what had ever given her the notion that he might accept her offer. If he wouldn't be hired by Kate Roark or the Cattlemen's Association, why would he take on any of her troubles? The idea had been a crazy one, that's all, an act of desperation.

"I appreciate the offer, Miss Cronin, but—"

"I'm sorry, Mr. Blaine. I shouldn't have asked. I know you've private business that brought you here—Brad Simmons said as much. It's just that . . . you're the first man I've seen who might have nerve enough to do what I ask, and not care what anyone else thought or said. And might make the others think twice about trying to scare you away." She shook her head, accepting defeat. "We'd be in the middle, like I said. And maybe that would mean they'd leave us alone, like a buffer. Like this hotel. There's never been trouble here, and Mr. Allison tries to keep it that way, so anyone can come here and not have to sit with his back to the wall. But like as not it wouldn't be that easy. All you'd have would be trouble threatening from two sides. I had no right to ask it of you."

"But you'd be there," Blaine said slowly.

"Yes." There was stubborn defiance in the assertion.

Blaine studied her with new appreciation. He had almost rejected her offer out of hand, but now he hesitated. It was not only that she was an attractive, appealing woman with a great deal of unassuming courage, or even the quick sympathy awakened by the story of her father's death in a fire—a fact that had a very special meaning for Blaine himself. These things had made it difficult to turn down her plea, but only that. Alone they would not have swayed him.

He was thinking of what she had said—that at the Paradise he would be sitting between the valley's warring factions, a presence impossible to ignore. And a tempting, highly visible target.

Ned Keatch would know who he was and why he was there. And Keatch might begin to think this was as good a time as any to get the bear off his back. If Blaine could be cut down, no one would be surprised. No one would question the deed. Keatch might even have some help, whichever side he was on.

Sooner or later, Blaine thought, Keatch would be driven to make his play. He might suspect a trap but, like a hungry animal, he wouldn't be able to ignore so tempting a bait.

"All right, Miss Cronin," Blaine said. "You've hired yourself a hand."

He saw both surprise and joy leap into the young woman's eyes. It did not occur to him, then, that his decision was hardly fair to her.

SEVEN

They left the following morning. At Blaine's suggestion, Nancy Cronin went alone to Anderson's Feed Barn shortly after sunrise. Anderson hitched up her team to the buckboard she had kept there in the storage yard next to the barn. Anderson was a taciturn man, and if he was curious he did not reveal it with questions.

She then drove the wagon over to Colvey's General Store. Ed Colvey was more openly curious, but he filled her order eagerly, loading the buckboard with supplies from rope and wire to grain, beans, bacon, and canned goods. Business had been poor all year, with many of the ranchers reluctant to come into town any more than necessary, and with many of them having lost their regular hands, those who saw little promise in being targets for lead pills when all they really wanted to do was punch cows. Colvey was not going to question a good order until it was filled.

It took him a long time, then, to ask the question in his mind. That came only when the wagon had been loaded up and Nancy Cronin had paid his bill in cash. "I don't mean to sound like I'm prying, Miss Cronin, but do you mind my asking where you're taking all these supplies?"

"It's pretty obvious, isn't it, Mr. Colvey?" she replied. And the next words brought a lift to her spirits that banished the morning's lingering worry. "I'm going home."

She climbed onto the seat of the buckboard just as Cullom Blaine appeared from the direction of the stables. He secured his buckskin to a lead behind the wagon and took his place beside Nancy, accepting the reins. Blaine clucked at the team and gave the reins a flick to goad them into motion.

As the wagon rode out of town in the long shadows of early morning, Blaine reflected that they were providing a staple of breakfast conversation for most of the town's citizens. And the news would surely spread from town across the valley at least as fast as the buckboard traveled—and probably faster.

The sky was high and brilliant, and the day quickly heated up. The valley Blaine saw in leisurely fashion for the first time confirmed his impression of it. In a good year this would be rich grassland, the kind that would tempt any cattleman to dreams of fat beeves and thriving herds, but now it was parched and yellow, the grass stunted and thin, a thirsty land where only thistles and burrs seemed to thrive. The wagon's wheels threw up a thick white worm of dust that climbed high against the morning sky, filtering out the sun's rays behind them.

They rode mostly in silence. Blaine, so long a loner, was not talkative, and Nancy Cronin was absorbed in her own thoughts. The sun climbed and the dust thickened along their back trail, climbing until it thinned out and was lost in the morning haze. They met no one.

Shortly before noon Blaine stopped to rest and water the horses at a nearly dry hole. Two hours later the buckboard rumbled across a dry wash and climbed a shallow slope. Blaine sensed the quickening of his companion's emotions. She sat up straighter, peering ahead eagerly.

When they topped the rise he heard Nancy Cronin's gasp. Blaine eased the wagon to a halt.

Art Cronin had built his home at the edge of a meadow within sight of a stream that emerged between two low foothills to the northwest. Giant oaks had sheltered the house, which was now a leveled ruin. Only a stone chimney stood upright amid the ashes. The trees had been blackened by the fire, which had spread to the surrounding grass, eating a short way up the hills behind the house and at one place even jumping the stream north of the buildings before it burned out.

The fire had occurred in the spring, Blaine remembered. The grass had been new. It hadn't burned the way it would now. Once started at this lag end of a dry summer, a grass fire might roar across the whole valley, as unstoppable as an avalanche.

Staring at the silent, desolate scene, Blaine closed his mind against bitter memory.

"I haven't wanted to come back alone," Nancy Cronin said. "I'd forgotten how . . ." Her voice trailed off. The mind sought to soften the harshness of so terrible a reality; in the time since spring she had come to remember this place not as she had last seen it but as it had been before the fire. Now there was no escaping the truth. Little of what she had known here and loved was left, except the land itself.

Blaine drove the wagon down the trail until Nancy Cronin asked him to stop. She climbed down and walked across the meadow toward a single huge old cottonwood that lifted above a small knoll. She stood there alone, head bent. Blaine saw the markers of twin graves beneath the shelter of the great tree, which had been far enough from the house to escape most of the fury of the fire, showing only some brown leaves and bare limbs along its west side, as if it had been seared by lightning.

His eyes bleak, Blaine drove slowly ahead toward the ashes of another man's dream, which he had so optimistically called Paradise.

* * *

That night Blaine slept in the open, having laid his ground sheet and blanket in the shallow depression of a little gully that in the past had carried the runoff from the nearby stream. And would again, he thought. A land's miseries might seem to last forever to the people caught up in them; for the earth itself they were brief spasms, one season's flood balancing another's drought, each no more significant than the blinking of an eye.

He was invisible where he lay in the shadows just beneath the lip of the shallow crease. He had chosen the place out of long habit. He would not be seen easily by anyone approaching the former headquarters of Paradise. He was expecting no one—not this soon—but his caution was ingrained.

Nancy Cronin had protested. She slept in the bunkhouse, the only building to survive the fire more or less whole. It was a long, low, and narrow structure built of heavy planks, scorched on the end that faced the house as well as on the long side nearest the barn. Flying sparks and cinders had burned holes in the roof, the windows were broken, and one of the two doors was off its hinges. But the building as a whole was solid. It would provide immediate shelter and, with a little repair, even make a comfortable living quarters. "I've slept under the same roof with Pa," Nancy said, "and camped out with him and the other hands more times than I could count. There's room for both of us."

"It's not the same," Blaine said.

She had accepted his decision rather quickly.

A good woman, Blaine thought, staring up at the countless stars. This first day had been hardest on her, but she had come through it with her head up. She was still unwilling to poke around much in the debris of the house for things that might have survived in usable condition, but even that would come.

Looking up at the brilliant immensity of the night sky, it was almost impossible not to accept some great purpose in its grandeur, but down here at the bottom of the well, where the smell of old ashes still clung to the slightest breeze, it was easier to see a blind capriciousness in the twisted lives of people. To Blaine it made no sense at all for a woman like Nancy Cronin to be alone, lying dry-eyed and sleepless in that bunkhouse. Or for a woman like Kate Roark, so vibrant and sensuous, to be consumed by the passion of hate instead of love. Their lives might have had no more direction than the black dust that drifted on the night air.

Like Samantha. She had—

He turned in his blanket, close to anger, shutting off the thought.

Perhaps he had made a mistake in accepting Nancy Cronin's offer. He had come to this valley for one reason only. Now he was in danger of becoming entangled in other lives, other purposes. This place cried out for the work of a man's hands, a strong back. There was so much to be done that he would have little time for anything else. Even a small ranch could consume all of a man's time and energy. And when it wasn't even his own. . . .

Restless, Blaine rolled once more onto his back. He couldn't back out now. Not after seeing the slow change in Nancy Cronin which had occurred even during this first day. What had begun in sadness had progressed to determination and, finally, just before he had said good night to her, a quiet acceptance, an inner peace. This was where she belonged.

It was a feeling Cullom Blaine could recognize, but it was not one that he ever expected to know again.

EIGHT

On the morning of the fourth day Blaine was able to look about him with a feeling of mild surprise over what had been accomplished.

The bunkhouse was intact once more. It had always had two rooms, one the cook's shack and the other for bunking down, eating, and playing cards. The stove in the cook's room was still serviceable, and that half of the shack was now a fairly presentable kitchen. The main room had been converted into comfortable living quarters for Nancy Cronin. The holes in the roof had been patched, the windows covered, one with glass salvaged from the main house, the other with improvised shutters. The floor was clean, all traces of dirt and ashes swept away. The broken door had been replaced with a newly made one, swinging on the original hinges.

Outside, there were other signs of change. The well had been cleaned out. It would need a new pump, but in the meanwhile the water in the nearby stream was potable. And the corral had been easily rebuilt. Much of it had been torn down, the destructive caprice of men rather than the fire, but the poles had been left on the ground where they fell.

On that morning Blaine saddled Randy, his buckskin. He had grown increasingly restless even as he worked. There had been a kind of surprise in rediscovering how much pleasure there could be in building and repairing, in using eye and mind and hand to make something solid and permanent, in seeing what needed to be done and, bone tired at the end of the day, in taking note of tasks completed, others begun. But even this sense of satisfaction, of fleeting pleasure, made him uneasy, like a Puritan discovering himself smiling at a barn dance.

"Are you sure you don't want me to go along, Mr. Blaine?" Nancy Cronin asked him as he prepared to leave.

"I'll find it."

"I've no doubt of that, but . . . Mr. Tucker hasn't heard from me in so long. He might take it strange I'd send someone else after my horses. And he doesn't know you."

"He'll know who I am," Blaine said dryly. "You can rest easy on that. And he won't have to be told I'm working for you now. I doubt there's many in this valley don't know that by now. I should be back by nightfall," he added. "If I'm not, board up and stay inside."

She nodded absently. "It's you going to the Tucker place that worries me. If Walt Hamill's there . . ."

Blaine grinned. "I'll stay downwind of him."

"It's no laughing matter," she said with a frown. "I . . . I don't think Walt is very smart, Mr. Blaine. If some of Tucker's men have been making fun of him, he wouldn't need much prodding to want to prove it was all a mistake. Isn't that the way men are?"

Blaine's smile thinned out. "Hamill was put up to that fight, after being pumped full of whiskey. Is Tucker the kind of man to stand for that on his own place?"

"No, but—"

"Don't fret about it, Nancy." He saw the flicker of surprise in her eyes, for he had not used her first name before. "If a man worried about everyone who might carry a chip on his shoulder in this country, he'd soon be so loaded down with worry he'd end up hiding in a hole. If Walt Hamill wants more trouble, he'll find it, no matter what I do. But I doubt he does."

"You're a stubborn man, Mr. Blaine."

"Yes. But no more than you." His smile returned, softening the remark. "Else you wouldn't be here."

They regarded each other for a moment in silence. Then Blaine swung into the saddle. Nancy Cronin looked up at him, a question in her eyes.

She voiced it without thinking. "Why are you here, Mr. Blaine? Why did you take my offer?"

"I had my reasons," he said, almost curtly. And she knew that he had said all that he would on the subject.

A strange man, she thought, not for the first time, as she watched him ride away. But she was grateful to him, and when he had topped the rise and dropped out of sight she was suddenly conscious of being alone. Completely alone, she realized, for the first time in months.

She shivered, a chill crawling over her bare arms in spite of the warm sun. It would be a long time until nightfall.

*   *   *

Tucker's spread was to the northeast of Paradise, reached by snaking through some low hills and climbing to a higher bench. Blaine stopped once, shortly after noon, to rest his horse and to eat a light cold meal, washed down with water. He let Randy nibble some water from his palm. The day was hot and it had been a dusty ride, but there was still a long way to travel, coming and going.

Setting off again, he reckoned that he was still an hour from Tucker's place when he began to have the unmistakable sensation of being watched.

He was not exactly sure what had kindled the feeling, or even how long it had been there beneath the surface of his awareness. There had been no warning sound, no shine of metal or drift of dust where none should be, but the feeling was strong.

Deliberately he maintained his steady, easy pace. Blaine did not believe in punishing a good horse. From under the wide brim of his hat he studied the terrain ahead and on either side. His posture was relaxed, most of his weight carried in the stirrups, knees more active than his hands. Nothing about him betrayed his alert scrutiny.

This was rugged country, where the land tumbled from the high bench to the lower valley. The intervening strip was broken into big rocks and irregular hills and bluffs, with the deep slash of a ravine off to Blaine's right, pink cliffs ahead on his left. He rode on slowly, only his shadowed eyes working busily. The sensation of being watched stayed with him. It had not been his imagination. A man who had ridden as close to the high line as Blaine had learned to trust his instincts.

His hunch was that the danger—if that was what it was—was still ahead of him. And his eyes kept flicking back to those pink bluffs, and to the rimrock overlooking the trail.

That was a good place for a man to belly down. He'd have a long view of the wagon trail Blaine had been following since he came upon it just before noon, confirming Nancy Cronin's directions. From that height the watcher would be able to overlook the trail in both directions without ever exposing himself. Moreover, he was in a position where it would not be easy to get at him.

Briefly Blaine considered the possibilities. If there was someone waiting above that rim, he might simply be a sentry, one of Tucker's hands or one working for another of the small stockmen up this way. In a territory as nervous and trigger-happy as this one, such caution was only sensible. All the same, Blaine reckoned that Tucker's place was still some distance away, and the Hammond ranch, the only other spread in this direction that Nancy Cronin had mentioned, was farther east. If you put out a sentinel, you did so because you wanted to be warned of any unexpected approach to your own camp. You might have him a mile away, but not five or ten.

On the other hand, that bluff was a very good place for a man to wait in ambush.

When the trail dipped to the right, Blaine saw that it followed the normal course of any wagon route, which was the easy way. A man on horseback might pick his way over uneven ground or through a fall of rocks, but a wagon needed more space and the trail tended to accept the way offered by the terrain. This path accepted the bottom of the canyon because it was wide enough, level, and unobstructed.

And along that canyon bottom the trail was in shadow. It was also cut off from the line of sight to that rimrock by an irregular step in the cliff side.

If anyone wanted to pick him out of the saddle, Blaine thought, he would have to do it now or wait for him to emerge into the open at the far end of the canyon.

Blaine clucked softly to the buckskin with his tongue against his teeth. They followed the trail, dropping toward the mouth of the canyon. Blaine watched the hard line of shadow as it drew closer. He was sweating, his shirt stuck tight to his back. Never once did his head lift toward the promontory looming to his left.

He reached the cool darkness and felt the sag of relief. His eyes lifted. As he had judged, the rim of the cliff was not to be seen.

Blaine reined in. The man on the bluff—if Blaine had not imagined him—was further ahead. Apparently he had a better view of the trail north of the canyon. He would have to wait now, watching for Blaine and the buckskin to reappear out of the shadows at the far end.

Dismounting silently, Blaine snaked his Winchester from its scabbard. He would not have many minutes before the watcher on the rim began to get nervous.

He set off on a steady run. There was a foot or animal path that looped around the bottom of the bluff, angling upward. Blaine's guess was that it had to lead to the top, perhaps circling around to make a gentler climb up the back side.

His hunch was accurate, rooted in his familiarity with such terrain and with the habits of two- or four-legged critters. That bluff was too convenient a lookout. There had to be easy ways to reach the rim and come down again.

Like most Westerners Blaine was not used to running or even walking far in his high-heeled boots, and he was soon laboring. The narrow, twisting path was so steep at times that he was climbing rather than running, forced to use his hands and arms. He was soon breathing hard and his heart raced—although this had as much to do with eagerness as exertion. After three days of plodding labor it had been a relief to get off on his own. Now the prospect of action, the sense of danger close and real, most of all the chance that the man who waited for him at the edge of the bluff just might be Ned Keatch, brought a kind of exhilaration.

The path circled a big rock outcropping, hugging the massive rock like a stiff collar, and of a sudden burst into the open.

Blaine stared upward in dismay. This side of the cliff, not visible before, displayed a long, open shelf, tilting down from the rim toward the point where Blaine had emerged at the top of the path. There was no cover, no way to cross that open expanse safely without being seen.

But a hundred yards away, lying flat, a man peered over the rim.

Blaine couldn't see much of him. A pair of boots, a shoulder, the peak of a tall Stetson. Not enough for a useful shot, and certainly not enough to guess who the man might be.

He started across the shelf, his thumb reaching for the hammer of the Winchester. The prone sentinel had not yet heard him. He would be scanning the gates of that shadowed tunnel, perhaps impatiently now, beginning to worry, aware that it had been too long a time, that his prey should have come out of the canyon.

Nearly half the distance covered. Fifty yards or so. A little more of the man had crept into view, the thrust of his legs and buttocks—

Trotting forward eagerly, weight on his toes, Blaine stepped onto loose shale. It had been hidden from him by a crease in the broad rock face, and he had no warning. His boot skidded, and he went down in a rattle of loose rock.

Sprawling, he lost the Winchester. His hands went out to break his fall, and he felt a quick cool slice of pain across his right palm.

The man at the bluff's edge whirled about, sunlight glinting off the long barrel of the rifle in his hands. Blaine couldn't see the face under the man's black hat. There was only a glimpse of drab and dusty clothes, a slight figure, a flash of mouth and chin, and then the spurt of flame from the muzzle of the rifle.

Blaine heard the spat of the bullet off rock. He clawed his Colt from its holster, felt the butt slippery in his wet hand. He snapped off a shot just as the bushwhacker tilted to his feet and ran.

The loose shale slowed Blaine's pursuit. It was a deep, wide pocket, and his boots floundered, scrabbling wildly for leverage. By the time he reached hard rock the surprised sniper had gained distance, racing along the bluff to the north. He turned and brought his rifle to his shoulder just as Blaine reached his feet. Blaine dropped again as a bullet whistled overhead.

He was aware of blood spattering the rock about him then, and of the wetness of his gun hand on the butt of the Colt, but he paid the fact no heed. Grimly he set off across the shelf on a pounding run. The fleeing man had dropped out of sight.

When Blaine reached the far side of the ridge, he found another path that cut downward, this one wider and more open than the track Blaine had used. It switchbacked twice and disappeared from view.

There was no sign of the bushwhacker.

Then Blaine heard the drumming of hoofbeats. The rider burst out of a patch of scrub oak and raced across an open space far below, heading west. Blaine lifted his six-shooter, knowing that it was a futile shot, but his thumb slipped off the hammer.

He looked down at his hand, feeling a vague surprise.

Falling on the loose gravel, he had caught an edge of rock as sharp as a knife. It had sliced clear through the web between his right thumb and forefinger, biting deep into the pad. The cut was bleeding profusely.

With his bandanna Blaine bound the wound, closing his fist around the cloth and wrapping it tightly to stanch the bleeding.

There was little hope of catching the escaping sniper. It would take Blaine ten minutes to get back to the buckskin at the bottom of the canyon, another five minutes or more to pick up the fugitive's tracks. Too long.

And if the man had only known, Blaine thought grimly, he wouldn't have had to run. It would be days before Blaine would be able to use his gun hand for anything at all. Weeks —if he was lucky—before he could grip and fire a gun with any hope of accuracy.

Blaine's eyes lifted, watching the dust of the man who had tried to waylay him. Who was he? A Flying-T sentinel? Not likely. One of Kate Roark's hired killers? That didn't seem to make much sense either. Not yet.

Without hard evidence to go on, Blaine was sure of the man's identity. Ned Keatch had tried to end the chase.

And it might easily have ended here, Blaine thought, staring at his hand in disgust. *Your mistake, Keatch. You ran too soon.*

* * *

He reached the Flying T within the hour. Emlen Tucker was a short, blocky man with a square face and a full black beard, bearing a resemblance to President Grant. He wore a permanently dour expression, which may have owed something to the heavy beard. He moved painfully, favoring one hip, like an old bronc buster who had climbed on one wild horse too many.

He knew who Blaine was without prompting. While his welcome could not have been called cordial, it was civil enough, and quickly efficient when he saw the blood-soaked bandanna around Blaine's hand.

"Bullet, Mr. Blaine?"

"Nope. Cut it on a rock."

If there were other questions in Tucker's mind, he didn't ask them. He called out his cook, who turned out to have had experience with wounded soldiers in the war. He cleansed the wound, grimacing at the waste of some whiskey, pulled the severed flaps of the thumb web so they overlapped slightly, and seared the flaps together with a hot iron.

When the cook had bandaged the hand tightly, using clean cotton strips torn from an old shirt, Blaine found that he could wiggle his fingers, but that was about all. The thumb was virtually immobilized. The hand was useless to hold anything he couldn't grip with his fingers.

Big Walt Hamill, who was among Tucker's crew on hand, gave Blaine an amiable grin when he emerged from the cook's shack. "You sure somebody didn't get his teeth into you again, Mr. Blaine?"

"Not this time. Hope you don't figger on takin' another bite."

Hamill's eyes grew round and serious. "No sir, that was a mistake. We didn't know which side you was on, is all."

"We still don't," Tucker said. "That right, Blaine?"

"But he's workin' for Miz Cronin!"

Tucker's question had had the ring of a challenge, and Blaine looked at him quickly. The fact that he was working for Nancy Cronin had earned him a civil reception from the stockman, and more, while leaving Tucker and most of his hands cautiously skeptical. Oddly enough, only Walt Hamill seemed particularly friendly. He saw things in simple terms. If Blaine was working for Miss Cronin and not the Rocking Chair, then he was a friend, not an enemy. Tucker was asking for something more definite.

"Looks like I'm kind of in the middle," Blaine said.

"That's a dangerous place to be." Tucker glanced down at Blaine's bandaged hand. "Especially for a man who can't use his gun hand."

There was a moment's silence before Blaine said softly, "Reckon I'll have to be a mite more careful then, won't I?"

He didn't give much away, Tucker thought, but there was something direct and stubborn about him that won a grudging respect from the rancher. Blaine hadn't let a badly cut hand turn him aside from the errand he had been sent to carry out. And he hadn't asked for help.

Abruptly Tucker said, "You're welcome to stay the night, Mr. Blaine. It'll soon be suppertime."

Blaine shook his head. "Miss Cronin's alone at her place."

Accepting this instantly, Tucker sent one of his wranglers to cut a half-dozen horses from the group milling around in the corral. Each bore the Paradise brand—the letter P with a crude sunburst pattern over it.

"That all of 'em?"

"That's the lot. Two others was never turned up after the fire. I doubt Art Cronin ever had more than a dozen on his string. If you lead that gray, or ride him if you want to rest your own horse, the others will follow him."

"Good enough," Blaine said by way of thanks. Tucker expected no more. "Tell your cook I'm obliged. If he's as good at cookin' as he is at doctorin', I'll miss that supper."

He started to fumble awkwardly with the cinch of his saddle, using his left hand. Walt Hamill quickly intervened, and he made easy work switching saddle and gear from the buckskin to the gray. He handled the heavy saddle as if it were as light as a woman's parasol. Watching Blaine's reaction, Emlen Tucker's dour expression eased into something almost like a smile. He had been measuring Blaine's size against Walt Hamill's bulk, wondering how this quiet man had handled the big cowhand in town. He saw that the same bemused question was in Blaine's mind.

But Tucker's habitual expression returned as he watched Blaine step into the saddle. No doubt the man had more to him than showed on the surface, and he had sand to spare. The fact remained that, by signing on at the Paradise, he might have bitten off a lot more trouble than Walt Hamill could ever offer him. And he had put Nancy Cronin in the way of that trouble.

"Do you know what you're doing, Mr. Blaine?" Tucker asked bluntly.

Blaine's face was expressionless. "What I was hired for, Mr. Tucker."

With a brief nod, Blaine turned the gray's head south. He had a long ride still ahead, and not enough hours of daylight to make it in.

NINE

The line shack, half hidden by a stand of spruce, was tucked onto a shelf at the head of a canyon. It was almost impossible to approach without being seen and heard long before the shack was in sight. Recognizing that the man he knew as Sawyer had itchy fingers, Clete Yeager called out ahead in prudent warning. "Sawyer? Comin' in!"

When there was no immediate answer, Yeager was not surprised. Sawyer was a jumpy one. He wouldn't show himself until he had verified the identity of any intruder with his own eyes.

That nervousness was the one thing that caused Yeager to be uneasy about the hired gunman. It made Sawyer too unpredictable. Hardcase he certainly was, yet he gave the impression that the sound of a footstep behind him would make him jump out of his boots.

And draw iron. Yeager had known many men like Sawyer. A loner, with a surly disposition that invited neither trust nor friendship. A man who traveled light, unburdened by any dead weight of conscience. And one who, somewhere along the line, had learned a deadly skill with his gun, the one thing in which he could take pride. Yeager had no doubt that Sawyer was snake swift—and quicker than a snake to strike without provocation. Sawyer was about as dangerous to have around as a pet rattler, but in a shooting war such a man could be useful.

As Sawyer already had been.

But there was no sign of Sawyer at the shack. Two horses stood in a crudely built corral next to the lean-to building.

Both approached the poles hopefully as Yeager drew near. He noted the Paradise brand on each. Sawyer's own horse was not there.

Yeager swore softly. Sawyer had been told to stay put. If he were seen by daylight anywhere in the valley, and recognized, his presence would raise questions that Yeager didn't want asked.

His own fault, maybe, sending word up to Sawyer a couple days ago about the man called Blaine. Yeager had known that Sawyer was running from something when he came to Antelope Valley, most probably from the law, and that Sawyer was likely to be a borrowed name. Linking him with the fugitive Blaine was hunting had been no more than a hunch, just solid enough to justify tipping Sawyer off.

Had he run? No, he would have taken those Paradise horses with him. And Yeager doubted that Sawyer would buck Cullom Blaine head on. More than likely he had been spooked just enough that he needed to see for himself what he was up against.

Ned Keatch. The name was familiar to Yeager, although he had never bumped into the man before this spring. Keatch had run with a bad bunch down Texas way. Yeager wondered what had scared him into running so far, trying to lose himself. Blaine wasn't that much of a catamount. He had put Walt Hamill down with a lucky blow or two, but a fine gun artist like Keatch wouldn't risk breaking his fingers on a stubborn cowman's jaw. He didn't have to.

Dismounting, Yeager tied his horse to a corral post. He speculated briefly about Blaine. The news that he had hired on at the Paradise had come as a surprise. Yeager hadn't told Kate Roark of this turn of events; she wouldn't like it. Her anger could be handled, but Blaine's action was a puzzle. He had given Yeager a wide berth in town when he'd been warned against staying in the valley. Then he had turned about and taken on a man twice his size in a brawl. Maybe it was facing a gun that he didn't like. Yeager had known brawlers like that. Still, Blaine hadn't seemed that eager to throw his weight around. Obviously he was a man with a grudge, and such a man was always dangerous. But Ned Keatch—who called himself Sawyer now, if Yeager had guessed right—should have been able to cut him down. What had made him run scared?

In the shack Yeager found evidence of Sawyer's meager breakfast. A thick syrup of coffee still stood cold at the bottom of the pot. Yeager turned aside with an expression of distaste and settled down to wait.

It was hot in the shack, and Yeager's wait was long enough for his annoyance with Sawyer to simmer, building toward anger. Yeager had looked too long for a setup like the one he had now, he had taken too many risks to let it all be jeopardized by a second-rate gunman who didn't have brains enough to steal jam from a larder on his own initiative, or guts enough to keep his back trail clear. When Yeager heard Sawyer's horse picking its way up the canyon, he decided Sawyer needed a lesson in following orders. Stepping out of the shack, he quickly found a place to lose himself among the rocks overlooking the ledge.

He let Sawyer ride right into the mouth of the trap before he showed its teeth. "Hold it right there, Keatch!" he called sharply from his cover. "Reach for leather and you're a dead man."

Sawyer's hand was on the butt of his gun before he froze, his gaze darting wildly toward the rocks. Yeager stepped into the open, his six-gun cocked and aimed at Sawyer's belt buckle.

He allowed himself a tight grin. Sawyer's mouth was pinched white, and when he recognized Yeager he began to shake. "Damn you! Pullin' somethin' like this—damn you all to hell! You lookin' to swallow lead?"

"You're the one that's lookin' down the barrel," Yeager said calmly. "And you can yell all you want, but take your hand away from that gun—now."

There was a fractional hesitation before Sawyer obeyed. Seeing it, Yeager knew that he had come very close to having to shoot. He had figured Sawyer right. His first instinct was always to reach for that gun. He didn't even have a rattler's sense to see what it was he was up against before he struck.

"That's better, Keatch. That is your name, isn't it?"

"What if it is?"

Yeager shrugged. "No matter. Exceptin' you was told to stay put. What have you been up to?"

"None of your damned business!"

Yeager had not holstered his gun, and he kept it leveled at Keatch's middle as he stepped down from his rock cover. "I'm making it my business. I don't give a holler in hell about this man Blaine and why he's gunnin' for you, unless he gets in my way. You had your orders to stay out of sight. Why didn't you?"

Keatch's gaze shifted, darting back to Yeager's gun. "I had to make sure it was him."

Yeager watched him narrowly, judging whether he had cooled off enough to make it improbable that he would reach for iron the instant he saw his chance. Deliberately Yeager dropped his Colt into its holster. Keatch stiffened slightly—but that was all.

Yeager gestured toward the shack. "Let's get out of the sun. You got some explainin' to do."

When they were inside, Yeager toed the room's only chair toward him and straddled it. Ned Keatch prowled the narrow cabin nervously. He was still jittery, either because of the way Yeager had got the drop on him or because of something else that had happened.

"Let's hear it," Yeager said. "What have you been up to?"

"I followed the son of a bitch, that's what," Keatch said. "I almost put him down." He stopped his pacing, clenching his fists in frustration. "He ain't human. I had him right in my sights. There was no way I could miss him, but . . ."

"You missed?"

"I think I winged him. I don't know—I'm not sure now."

Keatch told of watching Blaine off and on for two days at the Paradise, staying well out of sight. When Blaine had set off that morning, Keatch had followed. "He took that wagon trail north, so I figgered out he was headin' for Tucker's place. I rode on ahead of him. I had it set up so there was no way he could wriggle out of the hole, but he did. He knew I was there! He couldn't know, but he did."

"You make him sound like the devil himself."

"He is," Keatch muttered. "You don't know him."

"He can be taken," Yeager answered curtly. "I hauled him into the Rocking Chair myself, meek as a cub, but Kate Roark turned him loose. That won't happen again," he added thoughtfully. "What's he got against you?"

"He thinks I was with a bunch down in Texas that robbed him." Keatch's eyes shifted away. "They hit his place when he wasn't there, killed his woman, burned the place down."

"But you wasn't among those howlin' woman killers," Yeager suggested dryly.

"No!" The denial was automatic. "Don't matter if I was or wasn't, Blaine believes it. He'll chase me into hell, that's the kind he is."

"What I heard, Ned Keatch shouldn't have to run from no sausage-fingered cowman," Yeager said pointedly. Keatch's story explained Blaine's steel-eyed determination. It didn't explain the fear in the slope-shouldered gunfighter.

Ned Keatch drew taut as a bow, half spinning to face Yeager, but he thought better of the challenge. Instead, he resumed his edgy pacing. "You don't know him. He gunned Abe Stillwell down at Fort Smith. And there's been others. He chased a man name of Seevers straight into Sam Price's hangout. There's no way he could do that and come out whole, but he did. They buried Seevers and Price both."

Yeager frowned, his thick black brows closing together, eyes thoughtful. That didn't sound like the ordinary man he had caught sleeping by the south pass. But that man, he suddenly remembered, had almost turned the tables, even though surrounded by nearly a dozen armed men. . . .

"It's luck!" Ned Keatch said, staring past Yeager, as if he saw the specter of his relentless pursuer. "It's like he *can't* be put down. There's some things you can fight against, but that kind of luck. . . ." His gaze jerked back to meet Yeager's. "You won't have to worry about me no more. I'm clearin' out."

"Hell you say. What's that supposed to mean?"

"I said it plain enough. I'm not waitin' for that lucky bastard to find me." Keatch paused, a stubborn defiance creeping into his pale eyes as he regarded Yeager. "You owe me two months' wages."

"You haven't done a damn thing but sit up here for these two months."

"That don't count for nothin'! You promised me wages for stayin' put. And those two horses outside ain't fair pay for what I done to the Paradise, anyways. That's worth another hundred, easy."

"Nobody told you to kill Cronin. That was your own bungling. I'm not payin' extra for a man to be stupid." Yeager's voice remained calm, but there was a flat, unequivocal ring to it. "I told you you'd get paid when the job was done. It's not done yet."

Ned Keatch bristled at being called stupid, but he waited an instant too long before reacting, long enough for doubt to seep into his brain. In the narrow confines of the shack, he was not sure that he wanted to try his speed against Yeager's. There was an arrogant confidence in Yeager's eyes as he threw down the quiet challenge. Keatch had felt that same kind of cocky self-assurance at other times, facing other men. He didn't feel it now.

"Keep your goddamn money," he said sullenly. "I tol' you, I'm lightin' out."

"When I tell you, not before. I reckon Sheriff Toland might be interested in hearin' how you came out of that fire at the Paradise without even gettin' your hair singed. And this Blaine feller, reckon he'd like to hear about you. He must be real good at sniffin' out a fresh trail."

Keatch's nostrils flared, and he started to quiver. "You're pushin' me too far!" he shouted.

"No, I'm just lettin' you see how you got better reasons to stay than to run." Yeager's tone softened as he switched tactics. Keatch was right on the edge. "You're my ace in the hole, Keatch. Nobody knows you're here. You do what I say and you'll get your wages, and more. You want Blaine off your back? We'll take care of that, too."

The moment when Keatch might have braced him had passed. His eyes shifted, darting around the shack, mirroring the quick dartings of his mind. Blaine had him spooked for sure, but he was no more eager to challenge Yeager openly.

"How do you figger to dust Blaine off?"

"It can be done. I want him out of the way, same as you do. And he can't look two ways at once."

"Yeah." Ned Keatch weighed this, but there were too many arguments tilting the scales on the side of staying. He didn't like being crowded into a corner, but Yeager had offered him a way out and he took it. He essayed a nervous grin. "I scratch your back, an' you scratch mine. That about the size of it?"

"Now you've got it." Yeager relaxed, although he would not make the mistake of turning his back on Keatch. The narrow-faced little gunman wasn't to be trusted. The time would come, Yeager speculated, when he would have to make sure of Keatch in the only permanent way. Keatch knew too much. He simply hadn't realized yet that his knowledge was just as dangerous to Yeager as Yeager's knowledge of how Art Cronin had died was to Keatch. Sooner or later Keatch would think of it. In the meantime he could be used. "You can start your scratchin' tonight. I'm sending some of the boys over this way. You know Cronin's place best. You can show them—"

"Hold up there!" Keatch protested. "I been ridin' all day. I'm plumb wore out, an' so is my horse."

"You can rest him. You can use one of them Paradise horses, and you'll have plenty of time to rest up yourself. I don't want you to make your move too early. Let 'em get plenty of time to sleep. You'll go in—"

"Blaine!" Keatch cried. "He'll be there. I tell you, I won't—"

"You'll do what I tell you!" Yeager's warning was crisp and clear. "Anyways, he might stay over at the Flying T, if that's where you saw him heading. Especially if you winged him like you said. Mostly I need you to guide the boys in. You can hide off in the trees if that's what you want." This last had a note of contempt in it which Keatch heard. "But you worked that ranch. You can help the boys get in close, and show 'em where to go. Now sit down, for God's sake, before you wear out those boards, and listen!"

Reluctantly Ned Keatch did as he was told, listening in sullen silence as Yeager outlined what he had planned. A half hour later, buttressed by the knowledge that he would have six Rocking Chair bully-boys to back him up, Keatch watched Yeager ride off the way he had come. If he got his chance, Keatch thought, he might even take care of Cullom Blaine this night.

*   *   *

Kate Roark was standing on the long porch in the soft light of dusk as Clete Yeager rode up to the headquarters of the Rocking Chair. He left his horse with one of the hands and walked toward the house. It seemed to him that there was more than one emotion in Kate's face as he approached, even a kind of eagerness, but when he drew close there was only the cold, superior arrogance he hated.

"Where have you been?" Kate demanded.

"Checkin' around. Keepin' on top of things like I'm supposed to."

"And what good news do you have for me this time?" The question was caustic.

Yeager turned his head deliberately to glance around the yard, keeping her waiting, at the same time swallowing the impulse to retort in kind. Trouble was, she could always outmatch him in coldness or anger. All he had to do was look at that white throat, or the high thrust of her breasts, and something happened inside him, undercutting his normal reactions. "Maybe we shouldn't talk out here," he said slowly.

"I don't see why not. It can't be anything so—" She broke off, staring at him. "Oh, all right—come in."

The invitation was curt, almost contemptuous. As he followed her into the house, Yeager felt the dark flush of his temper climb the back of his neck. No one had spoken to him in his adult life in such a way, no one had lifted a hand to him or even raised his voice without eating his words, since the night, ten years ago, when Yeager killed his first man.

That man had been his father. He was a drunkard, and it was his habit when he came home drunk to take out his meanness on his woman and his three kids, of whom Clete Yeager was the oldest. From the time the boy was old enough to remember, he had been whipped savagely at least once a week, and had watched his mother take the same kind of beating, or worse.

The last time it happened Clete was seventeen years old. Bart Yeager reeled in from town, eyes red and glittering with the blind meanness that whiskey released in him, the meanness of a man defeated by life who had only one way to strike back. He had started to beat his woman just for the dumb protest he read in her frightened eyes. But this time Clete had picked up the old man's shotgun and pointed it at him. "Leave her alone!" he shouted. "Get out—don't you never touch her again!"

His father blinked at him in disbelief. "Why, you young pup! Turn against me, will you? I'll learn you to lift your hand against me!"

He started forward. "Stay back!" Clete warned him.

The old man kept coming, grinning wolfishly, and the boy pulled the trigger. The recoil against his shoulder knocked him off his feet, spinning him against the bunk behind him, and the thunderous blast deafened him.

Bart Yeager took the full charge of buckshot in the chest at a distance of ten feet. It kicked him across the room, almost cutting him in two. He moaned, "Oh, my God! Boy . . . !"

They were his last words. Clete lurched to his feet, driven now by a killing rage rather than fear. His mother was screaming, but his ears were so blocked he could only hear her dimly. He lifted the shotgun, looked into his father's eyes, and fired the second barrel.

Clete Yeager had taken his father's horse and ridden away that night, hearing the wails of his mother and his brother and sister, until distance swallowed them.

"Well?" Kate Roark said. "What is it you have to tell me?"

Yeager felt the slow sliding away of remembered anger, and with it the anger Kate Roark had kindled in him with her brusque manner. She was wearing a pale blue dress of light cotton, and it was obvious that the ripe body beneath the dress was unconstrained by any corsets. Sometimes he thought she wore such things deliberately, taunting him. Self-consciously he averted his gaze from the pale expanse of flesh at her throat, revealed by the deep scoop of her neckline.

"That waddy you let ride out of here," he mumbled. He cleared his throat and glanced at her quickly, surprising a cool smile on her lips. "The one from Texas—Blaine."

"Yes. What about him?"

"He could be trouble."

"I don't see why. He isn't involved in our fight. He's looking for someone—"

"He's hired on with Nancy Cronin at the Paradise. He's there with her now."

Yeager had the satisfaction of seeing Kate Roark's start of surprise. It was succeeded, however, by something that did not please him at all. Her cheeks turned crimson, and an unexpected fury blazed from her eyes. "That can't be true! He'd have no reason!"

"That's what he's done, all the same. They been at the Paradise these last three or four days." He shrugged, adding slyly, "She's been tryin' to get somebody to go back there with her all along. Maybe he took a liking to her."

"I don't believe it."

"Why not? She's a woman alone—"

"What would a man like that see in her? She'd have as much appeal to him as . . . as a wet dishrag." Kate paused, tight-lipped. "He must have had some good reason to go to Paradise with her. That man he's chasing—"

"He won't find Ned Keatch whilst he's mending fences and building a house for the Cronin woman. That's what he's been doing." The realization that Kate Roark spoke with more than casual interest of Blaine stung Yeager. "And that means she's back there to stay."

Kate Roark looked at him calmly. "You sound as if you know where this Keatch is."

"Why should I?" Yeager snapped back. "I never heard of him."

"Didn't you?" The woman's eyes were skeptical. "It

doesn't matter. But Nancy Cronin does, if she's back at the Paradise. I mean to have that grass, Mr. Yeager, and the use of that river. You assured me that it was mine to use. Now it seems that it isn't."

"It will be."

"How do you propose to do that? By killing her, the way you killed her father?"

Clete Yeager flushed. It seemed like every time they talked she threw that up at him. He was caught between anger and the desire she always awakened in him. That need was, if anything, stronger than ever tonight, made almost painful by the things the lamplight did to heighten Kate's beauty. It gave her skin the color and texture of rich cream. And when she turned, stalking away from him toward the fireplace, he saw her unfettered bosom tremble.

"I'm not responsible for that," Yeager said stiffly. "He was an old man. He should have got out of that house. I can't be blamed because he didn't."

"You can, Mr. Yeager. And we both know it." She regarded him coolly from across the room. Then, as if satisfied that she had made her point, she said, "You haven't told me how you plan to make Nancy Cronin leave."

"She's been scared off before."

"Mr. Blaine isn't a woman to be scared off."

Until that moment Yeager had intended to tell her that he had already taken the first step toward convincing Nancy Cronin that she was not safe at the Paradise. Now his mouth snapped shut. He turned on his heel.

"Where are you going, Mr. Yeager?"

"To see to my job."

"I'll tell you when to leave. And something else. I don't want Nancy Cronin hurt. As for Mr. Blaine, I don't believe for a minute he's at the Paradise for the reasons you hinted at so vulgarly. You leave him to me, Mr. Yeager. You seem to have your hands full trying to convince the other ranchers they can't fight the Rocking Chair." She paused to give the sarcasm emphasis. "That'll be all . . . for now."

She turned away, and Clete Yeager could only stare at her back, at the graceful line of her neck, the dip of her waist and swell of hip. Damn her—how long did she think she could keep him waiting?

"Good night, Mr. Yeager," she said without turning.

"Good night!"

He stalked out, baffled and frustrated, in what cowboys called a sod-pawin' mood. One thing was certain. He wasn't leaving it to Kate Roark or anyone else to handle the Antelope Valley War, which included taking care of matters at Paradise. He would do it his own way, without her knowledge if need be—and he would put Cullom Blaine on his back!

TEN

It was full dark when Blaine wearily climbed the low hill that overlooked the Paradise. A westerly breeze had come up to cool the night, and as he topped the rise, coming in by way of the meadow just north of the wagon trail, Blaine fancied that, even at some distance, he could smell the dank odor of stale ashes on the wind.

Or would the smell of ashes always be in his mind?

The bunkhouse showed no light. As he rode toward the shelter, Blaine made out the two wagon horses in the pasture. The string he had brought with him from the Flying T hurried eagerly down the slope, sensing the return to familiar territory. They had been no trouble on the long ride, which was just as well. Blaine hadn't been equal to any chase in the dark.

Dismounting, he opened the gate and led the gray through into the corral. The others followed in a rush. Blaine reset the gate and stripped down the gray. As he carried his saddle over to the side of the corral, using his one good hand, a shadow broke away from a corner of the bunkhouse. Blaine saw the shine of moonlight on gun metal.

"So you decided to come back."

The voice went with the tall, lean figure. Blaine slacked his saddle beside the bunkhouse step and confronted Brad Simmons. "You pointin' that rifle, or just keepin' your hands busy?"

"I was pointin' it until I was sure who you were."

Blaine checked his temper. He was tired of looking down

the length of a gun barrel, but this time Simmons had an argument. "Well, now you know."

Simmons did not reply, but the muzzle of his rifle tipped further away, pointing toward the ground. After a moment he said, "Those are Paradise horses you brought back?"

"That's right."

"I suppose you think it was a good idea to fetch them."

"They'll be needed, if this is to be a working ranch. Horses, and men to ride them."

"You won't find the men, so a damn lot of good the horses will do you, or Miss Cronin. And while you were off horse hunting, you left her here alone. Was that your idea?"

"Brad!" Nancy Cronin had emerged from the far end of the bunkhouse, now her living quarters. "There's no call for that. I wanted those horses, and Mr. Blaine was doing me a favor."

"Bringin' you here was no favor," Simmons answered tersely. "I've told you what I think about that. This is no place for you, the way things are."

"That's for me to decide," she answered firmly. "This is my home. I won't be run off it again. Kate Roark wouldn't dare try to burn me out a second time, anyway."

"There's no proof she was behind the first burning," Simmons said, but without conviction. "Nancy, I'm only thinkin' it's dangerous for you to be here. One man can't protect you. And he damn-all can't do it while he's off at the Flying T!"

"Well, you've protected me while he was gone, so you can just stop worrying about that, can't you?"

"What about tomorrow? And the day after that? There are too many troublemakers loose in this valley, just waiting for a chance to start something."

"I'd think you might be a little reluctant to bring that up, Brad Simmons. It was one of your troublemakers shot Sean Roark and brought it all to a head."

For a long moment Simmons was silent. He seemed

hardly aware of Cullom Blaine now. In the moonlight his long face with its lantern jaw was sadder, the shadows carved deeper around his mouth. "I don't need you to remind me," he said stiffly.

Nancy Cronin stepped quickly toward him, one hand reaching out to touch his arm. "Oh, Brad, I . . . I'm sorry. I shouldn't have said that. It wasn't your fault. I just . . ."

"You just said what you thought."

"If this is a private quarrel," Cullom Blaine drawled, "I'll just leave you two alone."

Brad Simmons jerked toward him, as if surprised to find him there. "That won't be necessary, Mr. Blaine. I'm the one who'll be leavin', now that you're back. Miss Cronin seems to think that you offer adequate protection. Well, I want you to know this. I'm not sure why you took this job, or how you think it'll help you find the man you're lookin' for, but you haven't only stuck your own neck out. You've put Nancy out here on the line with you. If anything happens to her because of it, you'll answer to me! I'm holdin' you responsible."

"Brad, that's nonsense!" Nancy Cronin cried.

"Is it?" He flung the question first at her, then repeated it. "Is it, Mr. Blaine?"

Blaine was frowning. He hadn't quite seen the situation from Simmons' perspective before. Now both Simmons and Emlen Tucker had taken pains to point out his responsibility for the young woman's welfare. There was some truth in the fact that, in coming to the Paradise for purposes of his own, believing that his presence there might draw Ned Keatch to him, he might have exposed Nancy Cronin to a risk that had nothing to do with her. Still, returning to Paradise had been what she wanted—her idea, in fact. Sooner or later she would have found someone with enough sand, or pockets empty enough, to ride with her. In Blaine's experience most cowhands didn't like killing. They would be glad enough to take a real job and leave the shooting war to men of a different stamp. If she could hold her place here with his help, and make it stick, she would be able to offer real work to men who were tired of dodging bullets. That might go a long way toward taking the steam out of the Antelope Valley War.

But, to be honest, that wasn't why he had hired on. Simmons was right. He couldn't dodge his responsibility.

Blaine felt suddenly weary. It had been a long day, and his hand had troubled him through most of the ride back from the Flying T. "If that should happen, Mr. Simmons," he said, "you won't have to look for me. I'll be here."

He turned on his heel. Let them wind it up alone, he thought. There was an undercurrent of feeling between them that didn't come out into the open, something he had guessed at before. It had nothing to do with him.

Moments later he heard the drumming of hoofbeats as Brad Simmons rode off. Idly Blaine wondered how far Simmons had to go to reach his place. It was late for the head of the Cattlemen's Association to be out riding alone, considering the explosive situation in the valley. One bullet from the darkness might take the heart out of the organization of small ranchers. It was a possibility that must surely have occurred to Clete Yeager, if Blaine's judgment of men was any good at all.

"Mr. Blaine?"

Nancy Cronin had followed him from the bunkhouse. Trying to leave her alone with Simmons, Blaine had walked over near the leveled ruin of the old house. The young woman paused beside him, staring at the black bed of ashes.

"Yes, ma'am?"

"I suppose you wonder what that was all about."

"No."

"Is it that obvious?" She paused. "I've known Brad since we were youngsters. A long time, Mr. Blaine. We . . . Kate

Roark and Brad and I sort of grew up together in this valley. We were all friends, once."

"You don't have to tell me."

"You have a right to know how things stand. Kate and I . . . I guess you could say we were rivals. It was always simply a question of which one of us Brad would choose." Blaine saw the wry twist of her smile. "You've met Kate, Mr. Blaine. I guess you know it was never much of a contest. I never had a real chance, competing with her for a man."

"I don't believe that."

"No? Well, it doesn't matter. Brad chose her. They were to be married. That was before Mr. Roark was shot. I think that's part of the reason Kate hates so hard, because she blames Brad for what happened. I suppose maybe she still loves him." Nancy gave a sudden, brittle little laugh. "If that sounds like I'm feeling sorry for myself, Mr. Blaine, don't believe it. I'm not a child, and I'm not fool enough to go on pining after something I can't have."

"He came here today."

"That's because he doesn't approve of my being here. Or you." She was silent for a while. An owl called from one of the cottonwoods near the river, but there was no answer. "I said we were old friends, Mr. Blaine. I'm sure he doesn't want anything to happen to me."

Blaine said nothing. He couldn't tell her that Brad Simmons loved her, because he didn't know this for certain, although he believed that it was a strong possibility. He couldn't tell her that she was just as desirable a woman as Kate Roark, because she wouldn't believe him. He remained silent, feeling the weight of the long day.

"Mr. Blaine—your hand! Why is it bandaged like that? I don't know why I didn't notice before. What happened?"

"Nothing," Blaine said. "Cut it a little, that's all." It would do no good to tell her that he had been bushwhacked.

After another moment she said, "I don't care why you came with me, Mr. Blaine. I don't believe you'd let harm come to me because of it."

"It could happen."

"Maybe. But it could happen without you. And you've given me what I wanted. You let me come home. I reckon that's worth some risk." There was a brief silence. Blaine stared at the dead ashes, a black smear in the night's shadows, and she wondered what was in his mind. "What did that man do to . . . to make you feel the way you do? The man you're hunting. You can tell me it's none of my business."

Cullom Blaine was tempted to do just that, but for some reason he didn't turn the question aside. Maybe it was because he had let down his guard, opening that closed door in his memory. Maybe it was because this was a warm and sympathetic woman, herself vulnerable and lonely, who had opened herself up to him with rare honesty. Maybe it was because, in the four days since he had accompanied her to the Paradise, he had found Nancy Cronin easy to like, a woman of humor and grace who reminded him of Samantha. Or maybe it was just because he was tired. Unexpectedly, without premeditation, for he was not a man who revealed much about himself ordinarily, Blaine found himself talking. "I had a ranch, like this one. I felt about it much like you do, like your pa must have done." He paused, finding it difficult to go on.

"You were married?"

"Yes. Her name was . . . Samantha. She was carrying our child when they came. We'd lost two others, and. . . ." He was silent. There were things he could not discuss with anyone, the private part of his grief.

"What happened?" Nancy asked very quietly.

"I'd gone into town for the doctor, and they must've seen me go and knew I wouldn't be back for a while. They were lookin' for money I was supposed to have. A bunch of thieves, lookin' for a fortune that wasn't there." His voice grew harsh as he talked, and Nancy Cronin had the feeling that he hardly knew she was there any longer. Maybe he had long needed this chance to lance the wound. "Eight of them there were, at least eight that I know of. And they had most of the night with her, tryin' to make her tell where the money was, and . . . using her. They took their turns. She was a . . . a fine-lookin' woman. She—"

This time Nancy Cronin dared not speak. There were tears in her eyes for a woman she had never known.

Tonelessly Blaine went on, as if, once having started, he could not stop. "When they'd done with her, and taken what little they could find, they set fire to the house." She was aware of his eyes bright in his dark face, glistening as he stared at the gutted remains of her own house. "They boarded her up inside. Alive. When I came she was still alive, I don't know how, inside that living hell."

Nancy put out a hand toward him instinctively, but she did not touch him. "Oh, my God," she whispered.

"I got the door open, and she flew out, like a . . . like a great black cinder blowing in the wind. Her hair was . . . she prided herself on her hair. It was a torch."

"Please, Mr. Blaine. Please . . . don't."

"There were eight of them," he said harshly. "Three are dead now. Ned Keatch is the fourth one I've tracked down, if he's here in this valley, as I believe. Keatch—"

"Stop! I . . . I understand."

She felt something go out of him. He was quiet then. When at last he looked at her, she felt a sharp chill. His bright eyes seemed to strike through to the core of her brain. His face was like cold iron, so winter cold that you might imagine that, touching it, your fingers would burn, the flesh tear when you tried to pull them away.

And she felt a sudden, unreasoning anger, a rage at the unknown, wanton killers of Samantha Blaine. With an intensity that surprised and shook her, she wanted him to find the man he hunted, one of those who had forged the winter iron of his soul.

Nancy shivered. Even her father's death had not taught her the depth to which her own emotions could strike. She wanted to reach out and touch this bitter, silent man, but she could not. He no longer knew she was there.

Quietly she turned away. When she reached the bunkhouse and looked back, Cullom Blaine had not moved, or turned his head.

ELEVEN

With the bunkhouse divided into living and cooking quarters, Nancy Cronin had encouraged Blaine to bunk down in the kitchen. So far he hadn't taken her up on the offer, and he decided that this was not the night to start.

He regretted talking so much. The effort, and the strain of confronting bitter memories that were probably best left locked away, had drained him. When he found a corner of the shallow gully near the corral and bedded down, sleep came with unexpected swiftness, sudden and total.

A crash aroused him, but his sleep was so deep that he swam out of it slowly. He heard shouts, hoofbeats, a woman's shrill cry. That jolted him fully awake.

The moon was gone and it was too dark to see anything clearly. There were riders milling about the bunkhouse. Blaine glimpsed two of them, carrying something between them. There was another loud crash as something rammed against the bunkhouse door.

Blaine charged out of the gully, rifle in hand.

It was reckless, a move that he might not have made if he had been clearer-headed. He did not see the riders to his left. There was a shout, a rush of sound that warned him to duck away, but he did not get clear in time. The riders carried a long pole between them, secured by their lariats looped around the pole near each end. Blaine missed the driving hoofs of the horse that almost ran him down, but his ducking movement carried him in between the rushing horses. An end of the pole caught him on the side of the face. It clubbed him to the ground, dazed and blinded.

He lost his rifle as he fell. Bewildered and in pain, he rolled instinctively, and by lucky chance dropped into the shallow cut he had left only a moment before. He lay there stunned, unable to move, hidden in the shadow of the crease.

Dimly he heard some of the noise that swirled around him. Someone shouted, "He went down there somewhere. Must be Blaine!"

"Where is he?" There was a rising note in this cry. "Damn it, don't let him get away!"

But in the blackness and the general excitement he went unseen. The raiders who had ridden him down had become turned around in the confusion and were not sure exactly where he had been. Someone plunged by within ten feet of him without looking in the right place. Blaine lay still, his head pounding.

There was another thunder of impact as a pole was driven against the bunkhouse wall like a battering ram. A board splintered. Blaine thought he heard Nancy Cronin's scream, but he could not be sure. He welcomed the pain in his head, for it was driving away the spinning blackness, pushing him toward full consciousness.

Blaine crawled along the gully as the dark shapes of riders hurtled this way and that, receding from him as they searched blindly, thinking that he had escaped them and must be running.

Blaine came to his blankets, and found his gunbelt where he had left it.

He dug for his Colt, forgetting the immobility of his cut hand. Swearing softly, he fumbled the gun from the holster with his left hand.

Turning, he faced the bunkhouse, crouching low to the ground. The right side of his face felt hot and swollen, and he could not see clearly. But in this darkness no one else could see anything, he thought.

A dark shape charged around the bunkhouse and flew toward him. Blaine fired.

The rider veered away, shouting. A streak of orange flame leaped toward the spot where Blaine had been, but he was on the move, running to his right in the direction of the burned house.

There was another shot, and someone cursed. "God damn it, watch where you're shootin'!"

"Where'd he go?"

Blaine scuttled through a vegetable garden grown wild on the south side of the gutted house. He waited a moment until he was sure of movement to the left of the bunkhouse, more than one rider there, bunched close together. He snapped off another shot, dug in his heels and ran.

He kept circling to his right on a route that would bring him back to the bunkhouse from the rear. The raiders had given up trying to batter the shack with their poles. Blaine wondered what had caused the first resounding crash that broke through his drugged sleep, but there wasn't time to ponder the question. Several shots exploded close together, their spurts of flame lancing toward the weed patch he had deserted.

Blaine fired again as he ran. Even if he had been able to see his targets, he would have had small hope of hitting anything, shooting with his left hand, but the series of shots from different places were having their effect. The raiders were shooting wildly and wheeling their horses in confusion. By the time gunfire answered Blaine's last shot, he was near the bunkhouse, a dozen yards beyond the path of the nearest searching bullet.

"That ain't one man!"

"Let's get out of here."

The darkness, which had covered the approach of the attacking group, had turned against them. No one liked fighting an enemy he couldn't see. They were in as much danger of hitting each other as the man they sought. At the first word of encouragement, several of the riders veered away.

One man tried to stop them. His voice was high-pitched, one that Blaine had heard earlier in the attack but didn't recognize. "No! Cut him down! Don't let him—"

The last part of the yell was swallowed up in the dust and drumming of swiftly moving hoofs.

Hard anger drove Blaine in a quick run to a corner of the bunkhouse. He was in time to see a horse and rider retreating past the corral. He brought his Colt level and squeezed off a shot.

A horse screamed and went down. Its rider's yelp held panic. Blaine could not see clearly what had happened, but there was more commotion as another rider swept near the fallen man. Blaine had one more bullet in the cylinder which had carried one empty chamber. He risked emptying the gun, shooting blindly, acting on the hunch that he had to keep them on the run. If they calmed down and turned back, there were enough of them to find him and cut him down.

In the dying echo of that last shot the rush of hoofbeats receded quickly. Silence settled behind them, dust and silence falling over the corral, the yard, the bunkhouse.

His head throbbing, Cullom Blaine leaned against a corner of the shack, his heart still racing, his anger high. He heard the horse which had tumbled struggle to its feet. It had been abandoned by its rider in his hasty flight. Someone was riding double, Blaine thought, cursing the loss of a horse.

He heard a choking sob. The sound drew him into the bunkhouse, where he found Nancy Cronin huddled in a corner of the living quarters. The room was full of soot and smoke and dust, and the woman began to cough and choke as he searched for her. He reached down, found her arm and drew her erect. "Come along—it's over."

She fell against him, sobbing. Blaine patted her shoulder

awkwardly with his bandaged hand. He still carried his empty gun in the other. He helped her out of the shack. In the open she leaned against the wall of the bunkhouse, gulping fresh air, her chest heaving. Even before she could control her breathing she was talking aloud, the words coming in spurts between her shuddering sobs. "Damn them . . . why can't they . . . leave us . . . alone? They'll pay . . . I swear it! They . . . oh, God!"

Blaine let some of it spill out, watching her, assuring himself that she was not hurt, only frightened. Her face and her night clothes were black with soot, and he realized belatedly what had caused the crash that awakened him. They had thrown a loop around the chimney flue and pulled it away. The rest of the pipe had collapsed inside the shack around the stove, releasing clouds of soot and smoke. It must have been a nightmare for her, he thought. Waking to that, and to the heavy battering against the door and walls.

He saw one of the long poles the raiders had used on the ground in front of the doorway, another nearby. He guessed they had come from the corral.

For the first time he realized that the raiders must have run off Nancy Cronin's horses. And his own.

Grimly Blaine looked toward the horse he had heard getting to its feet. It was important to know how badly the horse was hurt, since it might be the only mount he had.

He spoke sharply to Nancy Cronin. "Do you have a gun inside? Mine's empty, and my belt's back there on the ground somewhere."

The blunt question silenced her. She stared at him blankly.

"A gun," he said again. "If that horse out there is badly hurt . . ."

"You . . . you don't know that for sure."

"I'll find out. Get it for me."

After a moment her head nodded jerkily. She went into the smoky bunkhouse. He waited, looking with hard eyes in the direction the vanished raiders had taken. Not a killing raid, he thought, although that waddy with the shrill voice had been anxious to find him. The raid had been meant to create fear, to terrorize. To warn Nancy Cronin that she could not stay here safely.

She emerged from the shack and silently handed him a six-shooter. "It's loaded," she said. "I . . . I didn't shoot it. I never even thought . . ." There was bitterness in her tone.

"Don't blame yourself." He added harshly, "I should have been awake."

He walked away from her half-hearted protest.

He found the loose horse a few minutes later. It skittered away from him as he approached, but he talked to it soothingly, working closer as he talked. At last the animal stood for him. She was a chestnut mare with one white ankle. He caught up the trailing reins with a feeling of relief. Until that moment there had been the chance that the horse would simply put her nose to the wind and head for home, wherever that was. And if the raiders had indeed succeeded in running off the horses from the corral and the night pasture, Blaine would have been left on foot.

He left the mare tethered to one of the standing posts of the corral. The gate was gone, as well as some of the side poles used to batter the bunkhouse. Most of the other sections had simply been pulled down, destroying Blaine's work of the past few days.

As he patted the mare's flank before leaving her, he noticed her brand. Peering close, he was able to make out a P with a distinctive sunburst. Blaine examined her carefully. She was not a horse he had seen before, either attached to the buckboard on the ride from town or among those he had driven back from the Flying T. So one of tonight's visitors had been riding a Paradise horse.

He thought of the hand who had turned up missing after

the fire that spring, and of the two missing horses Emlen Tucker had mentioned. Coincidence? Probably.

What had that hand's name been? Watson? No . . . something close to it. Sawyer.

Thoughtfully Blaine returned to the bunkhouse. He found Nancy Cronin standing beside the open doorway where he had left her. The door to the living quarters, he saw, had been ripped from its hinges. One of the boards had splintered. The kitchen door was still in place, but it, too, had broken boards.

There was a rigidity in the young woman's stance, and when Blaine spoke she flinched, her whole body jerking. "That mare is fine," he said. "Shook up a little, like the rest of us." He looked past her into the shack. "The fire in the stove was out?"

"Yes." She stared at him. "I felt trapped in there. I woke up and I couldn't see with all the dust and smoke, and . . . then they started battering against the walls. I didn't know what was happening. One of the poles came through the window, and then there was shooting. I thought you were . . ." She shivered.

"Easy, now." He spoke to her as he had spoken to the panicky mare. "It's over."

"Is it?" Her eyes were wide, bright with lingering fear. "Won't they be back?"

"Not tonight. It'll be light soon. That kind works best in the dark."

"But there'll be other nights. They're not through. I was wrong, wasn't I, Mr. Blaine? Brad's right, I never should have come here."

"No, you weren't wrong. They're just trying to make you run scared."

"Well, they succeeded in scaring me." She gave a shaky laugh. "They've scared the living hell right out of me."

"Bein' scared is natural," he said gently. "In your place, anybody would've been scared."

"I don't know if I can handle it. That's what they wanted me to know." Her gaze jerked back to him. "You drove them off . . . you with only one hand to use. That was you doing some of the shooting, wasn't it? That's why you needed my gun, because you'd emptied yours. You could've been killed, Mr. Blaine, because of me."

"A man makes his own choices," Blaine said quietly.

She stared at him, her eyes still wide, and suddenly she was in his arms, trembling, holding on. Blaine stood there woodenly, stirred in spite of himself. Gradually her body stopped shaking. She continued to press against him, her arms around his body, her head resting against his chest.

At last her face lifted toward his. Her mouth was warm, eager, hungry. It was like kissing stone.

Nancy drew back. "How long can you go on remembering?"

"Till I've found them all," he said.

Shaken, she said, "I'm sorry. I don't know why I did that." She felt tears start, and fought them back.

Cullom Blaine's voice was surprisingly gentle. "I'm not the one you want. If he's half the man you think he is, he'll wake up one day—"

Nancy Cronin spun away from him. Shamed, hurt even though she knew that she had asked to be rejected, she turned and fled into the darkness.

TWELVE

In the morning Nancy Cronin was unexpectedly cheerful, as if she had made a remarkable recovery from the night's near disaster. Once, catching a glimpse of Blaine's sober frown, she laughed. "Don't look so worried, Mr. Blaine. I don't plan to hold last night against you. There's nothing so terrible about being an honest man."

"That wasn't worryin' me," he growled.

"No, of course not. It can't have been easy, having a woman throw herself at you like that. No, don't look at me that way, I'll say no more about it. It . . . was just something that happened. I'm not sorry it did, so there's no reason for you to go around long-faced. And that's the end of it."

Blaine wondered if it was. He knew that he had come far closer than Nancy could guess to responding to her kiss. But he also knew that a number of things had happened to bring them to that moment. They were two people who had been thrown together for several days in isolation, and they liked each other. But Nancy had turned to him because she had been badly frightened, he was there, and she was grateful to him.

And partly, Blaine thought, because of Brad Simmons' visit.

He saddled the mare he had found after the raid and rode off in search of the missing horses, having spotted one off to the east in the first light of day. Besides being something that had to be done, the action enabled him to be alone.

There was no place in his life for a woman. If there had

been, he could not have found a better one than the determined, freckle-faced owner of the Paradise. Simmons, he
thought, was a fool.

The incident had awakened for Blaine the emptiness of
his life, and the sharp pain of all that he had lost. During the
past two years he had shunned such reminders, steering
clear of intimate domestic scenes, of meals shared in a loving house, of the ways a woman could look at a man. Some
things dimmed in memory. It was better that way.

Within an hour Blaine had rounded up most of the Paradise horses, including the gray he had ridden, and—to his
considerable relief—Randy, his own buckskin. Either the
raiders had never intended to steal the horses, content this
time to cause trouble and deliver a warning, or they had
been unable to handle them in the darkness and the confusion of their departure. Only one horse was still missing. Either it had drifted farther than the others, or it was a trade-
off for the chestnut mare whose rider had been thrown in
the spill.

Small damages for so much trouble, Blaine thought. The
raiders had really been testing Nancy Cronin's nerve—and
his.

Returning to the battered headquarters of the Paradise,
Blaine turned the horses into the pasture and set to work
rebuilding the corral. It was a simple enough structure to
start with, and the poles were lying around on the ground
or, in one case, poking through the bunkhouse window like
some ungainly spoke of a giant wheel.

By the time he returned to the bunkhouse, he was surprised to discover that Nancy Cronin had managed to get
the stovepipe back in place, and she had swept out the
shack and washed down its floors. Soiled clothes and bed-
ding had been washed and draped over bushes to dry. She
had a blanket hanging and was beating it when Blaine
approached. Catching sight of him, she gave the blanket a

final vigorous whack, which produced a puff of black dust, and regarded him with a wide smile.

"Get it all straightened out in your head, Mr. Blaine?"

"I found your horses, if that's what you mean, and put most of them poles back where they belong," he answered amiably. "You're missin' one horse, but you've got that mare back, so that means you come out about even."

"What do you mean, I've got the mare back?" She glanced toward the horses in the pasture.

"She's wearin' a Paradise brand."

Nancy Cronin looked startled. "I don't understand. You mean one of those men last night was riding a Paradise horse?"

"That's the size of it. Mr. Tucker told me you had a couple horses missin' after that fire. That so?"

"Yes, but . . . what's in that head of yours, Mr. Blaine, now that you've stopped worrying about sweet-talking me?"

Blaine gave her a quick grin, which sobered as he said, "You had a man turn up among the missing, I recollect. A man and two horses."

"Yes, that was Mr. Sawyer." She paled visibly. "You think he could have been one of those riders?"

"Maybe. Maybe not. Could be that horse just got picked up wanderin' by someone who didn't lose any sleep over whose brand was under him." He paused. "What can you tell me about Sawyer?"

"Well, there isn't much to tell. He was . . . he wasn't a man you'd take much notice of. Truth is, I think he avoided me, Mr. Blaine. He was kind of a loner, stayed to himself mostly. Not as big as you are, and . . . just ordinary."

"He say where he was from?"

"Not to me. But he talked something like you, Mr. Blaine —like a Texan. What are you thinking?"

Blaine shrugged. It was a wild hunch, born of nothing more solid than the shrill pitch of a man's voice in the dark, a man who sounded scared when he was having all the best of it. It probably meant nothing. "Just that, when a man turns up missing and a couple horses get lost at the same time, you wonder. And when one of those horses turns up in a raid, you have to wonder some more. That's all."

"I see." She was pensive, turning this over. "It's enough, isn't it?"

"Probably don't mean much."

"But it might mean that Sawyer was here last night. And that would mean he was working for . . . for Clete Yeager and the Rocking Chair all along. He could have started that fire, Mr. Blaine. He was here—he had the opportunity. No one could figure how Rocking Chair riders got here that night without being noticed anywhere, and leaving no tracks."

"We're just guessing, Nancy." Blaine regretted bringing up his suspicion. Such speculation led nowhere without more tangible proof. "But they left tracks last night. They came from the west, but they were goin' south when they left."

"They came from the west?" She was surprised. "They must have circled that way, thinking they wouldn't be seen. The south trail will take them to the Rocking Chair, but there's nothing west but Paradise range."

"Anythin' out there worth tearing down?"

"No, nothing but an old line shack, and it's not worth tearing down. It's at the head of a canyon, hard to get to. They wouldn't have bothered with it, Mr. Blaine. And it's a long ways out of the way for riders from the Rocking Chair."

"We don't know that's where they came from, or where they were headin'," Blaine said quietly.

Her glance was quick. "Where else, Mr. Blaine?"

He was still pondering her question, and thinking that he ought to have a look at that line shack, when Nancy Cronin looked past his shoulder and gasped in surprise. Blaine spun around.

A rider was coming over the low rise to the east, approaching along the wagon trail at a steady but unhurried pace, sitting a beautiful black horse. But it was not the horse, spectacular though he was, that caught Blaine's gaze. Even at this distance he could see that the rider was a woman.

"I don't believe it," Nancy Cronin said. "It's Kate!"

* * *

Kate Roark wore a white shirtwaist with a coal-black open vest, divided riding skirt, and a flat-brimmed black hat. Her hair had been pulled back and gathered behind her head in some fashion for riding.

She looked down at Blaine and Nancy Cronin with a cool smile. "Well, aren't you going to ask me to cool my saddle for a spell?" she drawled, affecting a man's words and manner.

"Hello, Kate." Nancy Cronin's greeting was chilly, but she added, "You're welcome to get down, if this is a friendly visit."

"It is," Kate answered. "You ought to know I don't waste my time, Nancy. Or my words."

She stepped gracefully down from the black stallion, which did a fancy little jig for her then, as if demonstrating that he was still eager after his long ride. Kate patted the horse's neck and glanced at Blaine. "I heard you'd come home, Nancy," she murmured. "And that Mr. Blaine had hired on with you."

"Who told you?" Nancy asked, not trying to hide the caustic note in her voice. "One of your riders when he got back this morning?"

"I don't understand."

"I rather think you do."

Kate Roark glanced from her to Blaine, her gaze puzzled.

"I suppose that's supposed to mean something to me, but it doesn't. You'll have to explain."

"Oh, Kate, for God's sake, let's stop pretending!"

But Cullom Blaine had been watching her closely, and he had the clear impression that Kate Roark was genuinely mystified. Frowning, he said, "We had some visitors last night, Miss Roark. It wasn't exactly a friendly visit like yours. Seems like they thought they could knock the bunkhouse down with poles and generally stir things up."

Kate Roark's full lips tightened. Anger flashed in her eyes. "And you assumed they were from Rocking Chair?"

"Weren't they?" Nancy Cronin snapped.

"No! I gave no orders for any such raid. You're quick to accuse me, Nancy, just the way you were about that fire. But I didn't know anything about that fire until afterwards— and I know nothing about any raid last night."

"Is it so surprising that you're accused?" Nancy asked. But she was on the defensive now, taken aback by Kate Roark's forthright denial. Kate had seemed genuinely resentful—and surprised. "You've given me and everyone else in this valley reason enough for such suspicions—you and that gunfighter, Mr. Yeager."

"I wouldn't think you'd talk to me about gunfighters, Nancy. Your Association's gunman—"

Kate broke off, turning abruptly away. Blaine realized that she was making a strong effort to control her bitterness over the awakened memory of her father's death. Both women had lost heavily in this war, he reflected.

He wondered what had brought her to the Paradise today.

When Kate swung around to face them again, she was composed once more. There was even a faint smile touching her lips. "You'll have to take my word, Nancy. I sent no one here last night to attack your place. If I had, they wouldn't have been playing games. It's past time for that. As a matter of fact, that's why I'm here."

"I didn't think it was just a social call." Nancy seemed to have lost some of her self-assurance, Blaine thought. Apparently Kate Roark affected her that way.

"Why did you come, Miss Roark?" Blaine asked.

"You're one of the reasons, Mr. Blaine." She took off her hat then, and gave her thick mass of hair an absent pat and push with her free hand. A dusty ride had done nothing to cloud her beauty. Blaine wondered if Nancy was as aware of that as he was, and if that was partly behind her loss of composure. This was the woman who had won Brad Simmons from her. Kate went on pleasantly, "Do we have to stand out here in the sun? If your . . . bunkhouse isn't too badly damaged, Nancy, perhaps you'd ask me in. I didn't come here to quarrel," she added. "Or to deliver ultimatums."

Nancy Cronin made an effort to overcome her reluctance. "Of course," she said, adding with a strained formality, "Come on inside, Kate. You must be thirsty after such a long ride."

It was a while before Kate Roark got around to the purpose of her visit. Blaine suspected that she was, as she had said, a direct person, not used to mincing words or sparing others' feelings, but she seemed to feel obliged on this occasion to work around to what she had in mind.

Over coffee she pressed for specific details of the night raid. She seemed disappointed when told that none of the riders had been recognized or even seen clearly. Blaine did not mention the Paradise mare, and Nancy Cronin, guessing that he had a good reason for the deliberate omission, followed suit.

Finally Kate said, "Clete Yeager and most of my crew were at the Rocking Chair last night. A few were in town." She grimaced. "There was fighting as usual, and I have one puncher with a broken arm. I sent Yeager and some of the men to town this morning to fetch him and the others. As for the rest of the Rocking Chair hands, those who weren't at the ranch or in town were out working. I still have a ranch to run," she added pointedly. "Like I told you, I know nothing about that raid."

Watching both women, Blaine saw that Nancy Cronin, in spite of her reluctance to accept Kate's good intentions, was baffled by her obvious sincerity. Even the fact that Kate had come alone to the Paradise seemed to confirm her ignorance of the night attack. Blaine wondered if Nancy's growing uneasiness had something to do simply with Kate's presence in this bare, unlovely shack, so far from the elegant comforts of her home at the Rocking Chair, where Nancy herself had once been a welcome guest.

"I see you're both still wondering what brought me here," Kate said.

"It's a natural question," Nancy said dryly. "It's been a long time, Kate."

"Yes, I know." Kate's gaze was direct, and there was speculation in it that Blaine could not read. "Oh, I did want to see you again, Nancy. I guess you could say I was curious. I'll admit it surprised me when I heard you'd moved back to the Paradise and that Mr. Blaine had come with you." Her glance turned to him. "I offered you a job, Mr. Blaine. You said you had other business."

"I still do."

"I see. You didn't seem like a man who would change his mind overnight."

Blaine shrugged, wondering what she was leading up to. Direct she might be, he thought, but she was also subtle and clever. "You offered me a job carrying a gun," he said. "I turned you down for that reason. I didn't come here to take sides in a war, and I didn't hire on with Miss Cronin as a gunfighter."

"But you'll fight if you have to."

"I won't stand still while someone beats on me."

"No, I didn't think you would." Kate smiled. "But I don't know how you'd expect to do much fighting with your hand bandaged that way."

"He drove off those raiders last night," Nancy Cronin interjected sharply.

Blaine thought, *It doesn't take her long to spot a weakness.*

"Yes. . . ." Kate's glance flicked from Nancy to Blaine with new curiosity, as if she were discovering something she hadn't noticed before. "You're an interesting man, Mr. Blaine. I think you can do what no one else has been able to do in this valley, and that's to stand between the Rocking Chair and the other stockmen, and make it stick. That's what I want to talk to you about."

"Maybe you'd better explain that," Nancy said evenly.

"I will . . . to Mr. Blaine. And not here. I'd like him to come back with me to the Rocking Chair."

Nancy Cronin's reaction was openly hostile. "What are you up to, Kate?"

"Maybe it's time you stopped jumping to conclusions, Nancy," Kate Roark shot back. She recovered quickly. "I want no more trouble with Paradise. I never did. If you're set on staying here, and if Mr. Blaine is staying on with you, that changes things. Maybe it means it's time for a truce between us." She paused, her expression thoughtful. "You don't know how hard it is for me to say that. If you stay here, no Rocking Chair hand will take part in any raid against you. You have my word on that. But I'll speak plain. I don't want you here. And you won't be able to stay on alone." She looked hard at Blaine. "You need him. You know it, and I know it. So you're the real reason I've come a long, hot, and dusty ride this day, Mr. Blaine. I propose to give you what you really want—the man you came to the Antelope Valley to find."

Blaine stared at her, unable to deny the quick pumping of his heart. "Keatch? You know where Ned Keatch can be found?"

"It's a trade-off, Mr. Blaine," she answered coolly. "You come back to the Rocking Chair with me, and I'll tell you what I know. Because when you've done what you came for, it's my bet you'll soon be gone and out of my way." Kate paused to observe the effect of her blunt proposition. "I'll also promise to see that Nancy comes to no harm. She'll have safe escort back to town where she belongs."

"This is where I belong!" Nancy cried passionately. "And you needn't do any favors for me."

"Well, Mr. Blaine?" Kate Roark's eyes challenged him. "What do you say? You'll never find Keatch without my help, I can tell you that. Will you come with me?"

Puzzled by the offer, Blaine tried to dampen his hot eagerness, so that he could sort out his suspicions. On the face of it, Kate Roark's offer was startlingly honest and forthright. She was not apologizing for it or, apparently, pretending to any higher motive than her personal advantage. He could even accept the possibility that she might believe that his presence at the Paradise was a sufficiently troublesome barrier that she was willing to bargain to remove him.

Doubt remained. Perhaps it came from the very reasonableness of Kate Roark's offer. Cool, calm judgment was not a common quality in people long involved in a grudge fight. It didn't seem to fit the fiercely determined and vengeful woman Blaine had encountered on his first morning at the Rocking Chair.

But the bait she held out was, as she well knew, the one thing that could make him disregard caution or doubt.

Nancy Cronin spoke up suddenly, breaking a lengthening silence. "I don't believe any of this! I don't know exactly what you're up to, Kate, but you can't expect to come here out of the blue, after all this time, and have me believe you give a damn what happens to me or the Paradise. And I don't believe you'll keep your word to Mr. Blaine."

"That's for him to judge, isn't it?" Kate Roark seemed to become cooler, more confident and sure of herself as Nancy gave way to hostility and anger. "I know how you feel,

Nancy. I know what the Paradise means to you, and what you've lost. But I've lost just as much as you have . . . perhaps more. Your father's death was an accident. Mine was shot down in cold blood. I'll do anything to see Sean Roark's killers buried or dancing from a rope. You ought to know me well enough for that, Nancy. We were friends once."

"I know you well enough to know that you always get what you want," Nancy said bitterly.

"That's right. And I want Blaine out of this valley!"

"Seems to me like you're givin' me a lot more credit than I have comin'," Blaine said thoughtfully.

"I don't think so," Kate Roark answered promptly. "Not after the way you whipped Walt Hamill with the whole town watching, from what I heard. Everyone's still talking about that, and about the way you set yourself up here at Paradise with Nancy. Others will start thinking they can do the same. When they hear about you beating off those raiders last night with only one hand, you and a woman alone, it'll start a regular stampede." Kate's tone turned scathing and scornful, but there was also exasperation in it, as if she were recognizing that the little ranchers she despised could be far more troublesome once they stopped being afraid. "Every little two-bit rancher who's been scared off by the fighting will think he can do the same as Nancy. I don't want that to happen."

"You think that'll all change if I move on?"

"I do."

Blaine eyed her speculatively. "You can't be sure that's what I'll do."

"I'll take that chance," Kate Roark answered. "I know men, Mr. Blaine. And I know about hate. Whatever it is that's pushing you, you won't stop. Besides," she added after a short pause, "there's always the possibility that this man Keatch will be the one to ride away, not you."

Blaine was silent. She had thought it out very clearly. She had all the answers at hand. It was just possible that she had them because she meant everything she said. The truth was a hard thing to get around.

"Well, are you coming with me, Mr. Blaine?"

"Don't go!" Nancy Cronin cried. "Mr. Blaine, I know Kate. And I don't trust her. Forget about Ned Keatch. He isn't worth risking your neck for! If you ride into that nest of hired gunmen at the Rocking Chair—"

"I have to," Blaine said quietly.

Kate Roark's nostrils flared as Nancy's accusation rang through the hot, narrow shack—she had as much fire in her as that black stallion she rode, Blaine thought—but she kept her temper under control. There was even a faint gleam of satisfaction in her eyes as she said, "I'll get my horse. I can see there's no talking to you, Nancy. Mr. Blaine will have to make up his own mind."

She went out, leaving behind a prickly silence. Nancy Cronin looked anxiously at Blaine. "I don't trust her," she repeated. "Please, Mr. Blaine, don't go up there. Can't you see she's trying to use you?"

"Maybe."

"Would you walk into a cave with a bear? That's what you're thinking of. Clete Yeager can't be trusted, even if Kate could be. He's killed two men that I know of, Mr. Blaine, in what were supposed to be fair shootouts. Do you think you'd have any kind of chance against a man like that, with your hand not even fit to hold a shovel, much less a gun?"

"I doubt that's what Kate has in mind," Blaine said mildly.

"Kate, is it? I thought you hardly knew her. Seems like I've made a lot of mistakes lately, haven't I? Last night I made a fool of myself. Seems like I'm still doing it in broad daylight."

"Nancy—"

"Go on, Mr. Blaine! I can't stop you. Might as well both of us make fools of ourselves. But you'd better watch your back. I don't think Kate can control Clete Yeager any more even if she wants to—and I'm not convinced she does. You'd best remember that, before you strike any bargains."

"I'll keep my eyes open," Blaine said. "Will you be all right till I get back? I doubt there'll be any more trouble now, but—"

"Don't worry about me," Nancy said bitingly. "I don't need a one-armed man to look after me."

She regretted the words almost as soon as they were spoken, and she would have taken them back if Blaine had given any sign at all that he was angry or chagrined or wounded by them in any way. But his stoic face was expressionless, those strange green eyes unreadable, and before them she was silent.

Blaine spoke quietly. "If she wanted to get rid of me, she's seen this hand of mine that worries you. All she'd have to do would be to send a pack of her he-wolves. I have to figure there's some chance she's tellin' the truth." He paused, then added gently, "There's only one thing she doesn't have figured right. I'll be back."

"Will you?" Nancy's cry was bitter, despairing.

Blaine looked at her for a long moment before he said, "You'll have to trust somebody."

Then he walked out.

For a full minute Nancy Cronin did not follow. She stood rigid in the empty bunkhouse, her heart pounding, frightened because instinct told her that she was right in her suspicions of Kate Roark, and because she knew Blaine would not listen. He was a decent, honorable man, but he was also a driven one. Kate had seen his need for vengeance and used it, knowing that it would override any other consideration.

She went outside. Blaine had saddled his buckskin and was turning away from the corral. Astride her splendid black stallion, Kate Roark waited for him. Seeing Nancy emerge from the bunkhouse, Blaine touched the brim of his battered Stetson in an oddly courteous gesture. Then he kneed the buckskin and swung his head to the east, following Kate Roark.

Nancy stood there watching the two ride off until first Kate and then Cullom Blaine topped the rise and dropped out of sight.

She couldn't fight Kate with a woman's weapons, she thought bitterly, if that was what she had been trying to do last night. She had tried that before, with another man, and lost before.

Suddenly alone, more alone now than she could ever remember feeling, for since her father's death she had been sheltered from loneliness in the town, she had the despairing conviction that she would not see Blaine again. One way or another, Kate Roark would have her way, as she always had.

Slowly Nancy looked about her. This valley, which had been her home, seemed different in her sudden isolation, almost hostile. The hills to the west, with their green dress of cedar and scrub oak brightening the dry grasses, had always been a welcome buffer against wind and weather, a relief from vast reaches of open prairie. Now she saw only the shadows and creases, places of concealment, threatening and dangerous.

She thought of her father's losing battle to build a life here for himself and his family. She, too, had lost. With Blaine gone, there was no hope that she could stay on at Paradise. She could not stand alone against the angry guns of the whole valley.

THIRTEEN

On her spirited black horse Kate Roark set a brisk pace, leaving Blaine to follow along. It soon became apparent that she had little inclination for the two of them to walk along side by side, engaging in conversation.

That was agreeable enough with Blaine. Like most men who spent most of their lives in the saddle, he was accustomed to long silences. Often he rode alone, through lonely country, and even when he didn't, horseback was not a particularly good seat for conversation.

He guessed, also, that Kate Roark wanted him on her own ground before she talked. In that, she thought like a man, looking for any advantage.

He wondered what she had learned about Keatch, and how.

There was a strong possibility that Nancy Cronin was not entirely wrong in her suspicions of Kate's surprise appearance at Paradise. Blaine had made his decision to accompany her with his eyes open, recognizing the risk. He had concluded that, whatever her motives, it was worth finding out what she knew.

Blaine's cut hand had also affected his plans. It changed what he could hope to do. Trying to sit in the middle of a range war was hard enough when you were whole, ready for anything. It started to become less sensible when you couldn't even hold a Colt in your gun hand. He had been lucky last night. Lucky because the raiders' purpose had been limited, and because they didn't know he was handicapped. In the darkness and confusion it hadn't mattered that Blaine had little hope of hitting what he shot at. The raiders hadn't wanted a shootout this time, and it was enough that Blaine had been able to pull the trigger with his left hand, making noise and creating confusion.

He couldn't expect that kind of luck a second time.

That fact had made him more ready to explore Kate Roark's proposal than he might otherwise have been, in spite of his eagerness to find Keatch. But Blaine reckoned that he might have been curious enough in any event to want to know what she was after. She had offered to help him find Keatch the morning of their first meeting, but only on condition that he take a job with the Rocking Chair. What had really changed her mind? Or was she up to something devious? The possibility of an ambush crossed his mind, but he didn't take it seriously. His intuition told him that Kate had too much pride for that.

Well, he could sit his saddle tight and wait her out. She would talk when she was ready.

Kate Roark led him along a different trail than he had followed before. It cut across a neck of the valley and climbed steeply. A more challenging track than the one Blaine had taken in his descent from the Rocking Chair with Yeager and the other members of his crew. There were abrupt climbs and dips as the trail snaked upward through broken terrain. The route was shorter, Blaine judged, which explained Kate Roark's choice of it well enough. But he suspected that she also relished challenges—and enjoyed testing others as she tested herself and her horse.

Along the trail the signs of drought persisted. Lack of rain had created poor pasture everywhere in what would have been lush grassland during any normal season. Parched and dusty, the land looked harsher and more unforgiving. There was beauty in it even now, and grandeur. Blaine could see how it had both challenged and tempted Sean Roark.

From the empire he had tried to carve, the house he had built, even the daughter he had raised, Blaine had formed a picture of the dead man, Kate's father. A tough, hard, demanding man, the kind who wouldn't yield an inch of ground to either man or nature, once he had taken it. Undoubtedly he had never thought of himself as ruthless or a bad man. He had built something from nothing and felt that it all belonged to him. It was both a natural feeling and an inevitable source of conflict, for sooner or later other men had to come, many of them lesser men but each with his own cravings for land and independence. Sean Roark would have believed them all to be usurpers, scavengers on *his* land, eager to feed on his kill. Blaine had seen it all too many times before.

The land was challenge enough. Holding a place on it, in battle with the elements, was never easy. Man didn't need his own kind to fight against.

A man like Roark must have felt a kind of disdain for the quick gunmen who had come to the valley, even those he had hired himself. Surely he would have had a grudging respect for the smaller ranchers, even as he fought their encroachments. In their own ways they were men like him. The outlaws with their cold-blooded skills were the real parasites. They created nothing. They built nothing. They left nothing behind them except grief. They could only kill.

Like Ned Keatch.

Thought of the fugitive invariably brought a quick, reflex knotting to Blaine's belly. He didn't allow himself to think about Keatch too much, any more than he permitted himself to dwell on other memories that would inevitably bring Samantha to painful life. It was better to keep that door closed.

Idly Blaine kept flexing the fingers of his right hand. Nancy Cronin had wrapped the hand in a fresh bandage, leaving the fingers free. The palm was tightly covered, the thumb largely immobilized, the hand generally cumbersome to use. But he could pull a trigger with his fingers. What this

meant was that, while he could do little more than make
noise with his Colt, he could handle a rifle if he had to.

He wondered how quickly word would reach Ned Keatch
about the bandaged gun hand. That might encourage him to
make his play. The thought brought a tightening to Blaine's
chest, a hard eagerness.

Blaine put the gunman out of his mind. He looked ahead,
aware of the supple line of Kate Roark's back, the careless
ease with which she handled her black horse, accepting
these random perceptions as he accepted the afternoon's
heat and the dust and the vastness of the land all about him,
a stubbornly patient man who was willing to wait for whatever lay ahead.

* * *

They came to the Rocking Chair late in the afternoon.
The sun was still above the highest peaks of the Towers to
the west, but the shadows were long across the verdant
table where Sean Roark had built his fine, big, timbered
house. Blaine took in the layout with a closer attention than
he had given it before, seeing a cattleman's careful attention
to detail, from corral and pasture to calf pens, barn and tool
shed, blacksmith shop and bunkhouse.

It struck him there were few men about. For such a large,
impressive ranch headquarters, it was surprisingly idle.

Dismounting, Kate Roark called over one of the men
watching her from in front of the bunkhouse. Blaine recognized Walden, the gray-bearded hand who had treated him
with less hostility than most of Clete Yeager's crew. Walden's glance at Blaine was brief, his bland brown eyes not
quite hiding curiosity.

"Mr. Walden," Kate Roark said without preamble, "I'd
like to ask you about the crew. I'd like to know where they
are."

"Well, Miss Roark, you sent Yeager into town—"

"I know about him and the men with him. What about
the others? How many are here right now?"

"About nine, ten of us, I reckon. Let me see. . . ."

"You don't have to count on your fingers, Mr. Walden," Kate said impatiently. "That's close enough. Now I want to know who's been away. I especially want to know about last night. Was the whole crew here?"

"Well, no." Walden looked uneasy with these questions. He had been chewing tobacco, and he looked as if he didn't know where to spit, but Blaine didn't think that was the problem that worried him. "There's a half dozen been off in the Timbers for the past week rounding up. And a couple was out fence ridin' yesterday, and they'll be gone another day or so. Then Yeager sent a bunch out to the west range yesterday. They—"

"They're back?" Kate Roark cut in sharply.

"No, ma'am. I ain't seen 'em yet."

"I see." Kate glanced briefly at Blaine, who had been silently taking in this exchange. "When exactly did they leave, Mr. Walden?"

"Well, it was late on. I figured Yeager wanted 'em on the job come mornin'." Walden shifted the cud in his cheek. "You want to know what they was sent for, you'll have to ask Yeager."

"I'll do that, Mr. Walden." She turned abruptly to Blaine. "Nothing is proved, Mr. Blaine. We have cattle on that range to look after."

His face expressionless, Blaine merely nodded.

Kate Roark said, "Thank you, Mr. Walden, that'll be all. Take care of my horse and Mr. Blaine's. Come along to the house, Mr. Blaine."

She had acquired the habit of giving orders, Blaine thought as he followed her to the house. The curtness of tone had probably been unintentional, but the assumption that he would unquestioningly do what she said was simply habit.

The house was cool in spite of the day's heat. A woman with Indian or Mexican heritage in her black eyes and brown skin appeared. Kate spoke to her briefly before turning to face Blaine.

"You ready to talk about it now?" he drawled.

She gave him a long look. "After supper, Mr. Blaine, if that is all right with you. You'll have time to wash up, and—" Her mouth relaxed in a friendly smile. "I'd like to freshen up after that ride, get some of the dust out of my hair and my teeth. Maria is a fine cook, Mr. Blaine. I'm sure you'll enjoy supper."

Unstated was the fact that she had planned on their dining together. Alone, Blaine guessed. He wondered when Clete Yeager was due back from town, and if Kate Roark had planned for him to be away.

He murmured, "Seems like you're always feedin' me, Miss Roark."

"Is that so bad? Or are you afraid I'm fattening you up for the kill?" Her smile broadened, and there was a mocking light in the clear blue eyes. "Is that what you think?"

"It hadn't occurred to me, but . . . I reckon I'll have to see to it I don't eat too much."

Kate Roark laughed. She whirled away, skipping in an almost girlish fashion as she crossed the long room toward the bedroom wing. At the doorway she looked back. Her eyes were bright, but no longer mocking. "You've come a long way on just my word, Mr. Blaine. I think I can promise you one thing. You won't be disappointed."

* * *

The meal was a feast. In addition to a huge slab of prime beef, there were fresh vegetables, berries, bread, and cheeses, with wine to wash it down. It was served at the long harvest table by lamplight, but Kate Roark did not allow the length of the table to come between her and her guest. She had Maria set the two places at one end of the table.

Kate had changed into a dress of dark green velvet that

set off her hair and the rich cream of her neck and shoulders. The perfumed air and the softness of the evening
might have been as carefully planned as the evening itself,
not only to enhance the woman's beauty but also to impress
Cullom Blaine with a feeling of luxurious well-being.

A man could get to like dining with such a woman in a
place like this, Blaine mused. Trouble was, that impression
had also been planned. Like the low-cut bodice of her gown,
the red-lipped smile, and frequent ripples of laughter, it was
too calculated. Blaine thought of the Indian way of breaking
a horse without ever climbing on his back, just by gentle
handling and sweet talking all the fight out of him over a
period of time. By the time the horse felt the weight of his
rider for the first time, it was too late to change his mind.

"What are you smiling at, Mr. Blaine?"

"Nothin' in particular. It's been a meal to smile over."

She laughed. "I'd almost forgotten how close-mouthed
you are. You'll tell me only what you want to tell."

Blaine said, "You haven't exactly been in a hurry to get to
the point of this visit."

"It's time, isn't it?" She rose from the table, carrying her
cup of coffee with her. "Bring your coffee with you, Mr.
Blaine. We'll sit by the fire. We're high enough for the eve-
nings to get cool, and I like a fire."

He trailed her into the long room, where they took chairs
facing each other on either side of the fireplace. Kate Roark
regarded him over her cup for a moment, took a sip, and
then set the cup down with an air of resolution. "I guess I
owe you and Nancy an apology, Mr. Blaine. You heard what
Walden said. It seems that some of my crew might have
been away from here at the time Paradise was attacked last
night. They could have been involved, but if they were it
was without my knowledge or approval. I can only ask you
to believe me. If it happened, it was Clete Yeager's
doing."

"He works for you.".

Her tone hardened as she said, "It won't happen again. Not without my orders." Pausing deliberately, she leaned back, pressing her shoulders against the leather of the high-backed chair, a gesture that did nothing to minimize the swell of her half-exposed bosom. "I don't know how much you know about the Rocking Chair, Mr. Blaine, but it's the biggest spread in this part of the country. It used to be the best run, when my father was alive. I want it that way again. I need someone to run it for me—someone I can depend on. Oh, the men will take orders from me, they know better than not to. But I need a real riding boss. The men are uncomfortable when I'm around giving orders. They wouldn't know what to do with me along on the work of a roundup or a drive. I can't bed down with them on the upper range, or drink with them in the Palace. Anyway, they'd take orders better from a man, even though they knew those orders came from me."

"You've got Yeager."

"Yes." Her gaze was level, unflinching. "But he's only good for one thing, and you know it."

It was in Blaine's mind to suggest that she didn't have to keep him on, but he didn't say it. It might not even be true. He wondered if, as Nancy Cronin had suggested, Kate could get rid of the gunfighter easily now even if she wanted to.

As if she had read the question, Kate Roark addressed it. "I don't like Clete Yeager, Mr. Blaine. He's arrogant and he doesn't like to follow orders. He's here because the Cattlemen's Association wanted a fight, and that's the one thing he's good for." Setting down her coffee, she rose and stood before the fireplace, pausing to stare for a moment at the crackling logs. When she swung again to face Blaine, he was aware that she chose her words very carefully. "Once the fighting is over, Yeager won't belong here. He'll be of no use to the Rocking Chair. He's not a cattleman. Most of the crew who were here before he came, the real punchers, don't like him. They take orders from him only because they know they have to. For now."

Blaine made no comment. It had been clear to him for some time what she was leading up to, but he remained puzzled. Why had she chosen him? And what had made her think he would accept the job?

She couldn't believe otherwise, he thought. It seemed probable that no one, her father included, had ever been able to refuse her anything she really set out to get.

Heading her off, Blaine reminded her of what she had said back at the Paradise. "This isn't what we talked about before, or why I'm here."

Kate Roark shrugged. "I meant part of what I said—that I believe you might be able to stand between the two sides and make it stick. I don't want you there, Mr. Blaine. I can't allow it. That's why I wanted you to come back with me."

Blaine's steady gaze bored into her. "What about the rest of it? You said you knew where Ned Keatch could be found."

Kate Roark laughed. "Did you really believe me? Or did you come even though you knew it wasn't true?"

Blaine rose slowly from his chair. It had been a long chance, but he felt a surge of bitterness over being tricked. "I hoped it wasn't a lie."

He saw a quick stain of color in Kate's cheeks, but she held her smile and her voice was teasing as she said, "I had to say something to get you to come with me." When Blaine turned away, angrily searching for his hat, the woman moved quickly to block him. She stepped close to him, reaching out lightly to touch his chest, as if she meant to push him back. "We can find out, if that's what you really want. But listen to me, Blaine! You can't go on chasing ghosts forever, or whatever it is you're doing. Do you know what I'm offering you? Do you know what it would mean to boss the Rocking Chair?"

"If all you brought me here for was to offer me a job, you

already have my answer. I told you once before—"

"You took a job at the Paradise," she cut in swiftly.

"That was different."

"Because Nancy Cronin didn't hire you as a fighter? You still fought for her last night, didn't you? And you'd do the same again." When she saw the stubborn protest in Blaine's eyes she held up one hand to silence him. "All right, that was forced on you. But the point is, you hired on, for whatever reason. I'm making you a much better offer, Mr. Blaine. And I'm not asking you to ride herd on a bunch of gunfighters. Have I said that? I'm talking about when this fight is over. I'm talking about coming to the Rocking Chair as my range boss!"

"Does Clete Yeager know?" Blaine asked softly.

"He doesn't have to know! I decide for myself!"

Blaine looked at her intently, hearing the pride in her voice and seeing it in her eyes, in her defiant stance. She was a stunningly beautiful woman, he thought, not least when she was angry. It was easy to imagine what she might be like when another passion seized her.

She eased closer to him, until he could feel the warmth of her body and drink in the heady scent of her. Her face was lifted toward his, and the full red lips were parted. "Do I have to speak plainer, Cullom Blaine?" She drew in a deep breath, her bosom lifting. "Are you sure you found everything you want at the Paradise?"

"I don't understand."

"I think you do. I'm not a child, Mr. Blaine, and I have eyes and ears. Oh, I'm not throwing stones. You and Nancy were alone at that little place, in the bunkhouse together." She gave a little laugh. "I wouldn't blame Nancy for . . . anything. You're an unusual man, and she's . . . alone."

"You think that's why I was there?"

"Isn't it? You weren't looking for Ned Keatch at the Paradise."

"No. I was waitin' for him to come to me. I think he will,

sooner or later, if he's in this valley. He won't be able to stay away." Blaine paused, suddenly realizing that he did not particularly like this woman. He had to wonder if the promise of her eyes and body was any more honest than her words had been. The contrast with Nancy Cronin was striking. Whatever combination of fear and loneliness and gratitude had pushed Nancy into his arms last night, she had not been trying to bribe him. Or to deceive him.

Blaine's voice was cold as he said, "Miss Roark, did you come to take me away from the Paradise because you couldn't stand the notion that Nancy Cronin had a man you thought you could take away from her?"

Quick anger blazed in her eyes. "She's told you about Brad Simmons!" Her eyes narrowed and her breath caught as she struggled for control. "Yes, I took Brad from her. No, that's not exactly true—she never had him to be taken away. But that was before I knew what kind he was. Before he had my father killed! It has nothing to do with what I'm offering you."

"I doubt Simmons gave any such order," Blaine said quietly. "Any more than you ordered those men of yours to raid Paradise last night. Anyway, you're right, that has nothin' to do with you and me. And I think we've said about all we have to say to each other."

"Are you afraid of Yeager? Is that it?"

Ignoring the taunt, Blaine spotted his hat and headed toward it. Over his shoulder he said curtly, "Thanks for supper."

"Do you realize what you're turning down, Mr. Blaine?" she called after him angrily. "If you were half the man I took you for—"

Blaine whirled, his bright glance striking her so hard that it cut off her jibe. "What makes you think you can win any man worth having with a lie? Lies breed more lies, nothing else. Good night, Miss Roark."

He banged the door on his way out. He was halfway

across the yard, heading toward the corral beyond the bunkhouse, when he heard the door open behind him and Kate Roark's voice rang through the early darkness. "Mr. Walden! Lee! Smitty! Stop him!"

Blaine halted abruptly. He had shifted his holster around to the left so that he could grab his Colt with that hand, but the movement would be clumsy and slow. The men appeared from the shadows so quickly that he knew they had been alerted beforehand. Kate Roark had not bet all her stake on one play of the cards. She had been prepared for Blaine's refusal.

There were seven or eight men, all with six-guns or rifles carried in their hands, cocked and ready to shoot.

Kate's voice was harsh. "You know what to do, Mr. Walden. Lock him in the tool shed. And I want it guarded!"

Cullom Blaine held motionless, letting his own swift anger die away, leaving its residue of self-disgust. Hate could blind a man as readily as it could a woman, he thought. He and Kate Roark were far different people, but they shared this one dark emotion. It had given her the insight and understanding to turn Blaine's hate against him. That was a bitter thing to know.

FOURTEEN

Kate Roark prowled the big house, angry as much with herself as she was with Blaine. She had made a fool of herself, and that knowledge rankled even more than Blaine's turndown. He was just another drifter who had lost whatever ambition he ever had. He might have been useful, but she didn't really need him.

She poured herself another glass of wine from the bottle left on the dining table, drank it quickly, poured another glass, and carried it the length of the main room. She caught a glimpse of herself in the round mirror in the golden eagle frame and stopped, staring at the image of the woman in the glass as if she were a stranger, seeing the green dress that set off her white neck and shoulders, the hair brushed to a rich gloss and carefully gathered at the nape of her neck, the frustrated eyes and sullen mouth. In sudden fury she hurled the wine glass at the mirror. It missed and shattered against the whitewashed wall, spilling a blood-dark stain that ran swiftly down the wall toward the floor.

Maria appeared immediately, and Kate's anger found another outlet. "Get out!" she shouted. "When I want you, I'll ring for you, do you hear?"

Frightened, Maria retreated into the kitchen.

Kate took Cullom Blaine's empty glass from the table and poured more of the red wine into it. She was aware that she had already drunk more than she was accustomed to, but her restlessness made her reckless. She carried the glass with her to the front window, where she stood looking out over the porch to the gloom of the yard. There was a light in the bunkhouse, a lantern lit outside and another lantern glowing down by the corral. A shadow moved across the farthest of these lights. She thought she could hear the low murmur of voices. What were the men talking about? Her? And Blaine?

She glared at the tool shed, a small building dimly visible near the stables and the blacksmith's shop. *You made your choice, Mr. Blaine. Now you can think about what you lost. And when Clete Yeager comes—*

She broke off the thought, for it brought an unanticipated chill.

She had not told Yeager what she planned to do. She had not wanted him to know, and the truth was that she had never believed that Blaine would ultimately turn her down. Not after all she had offered him, all she had promised. When Yeager returned and found out—if he guessed what she had been up to—he would be furious. She knew him well enough for that. Knew, too, how much he wanted her. It was not merely a monthly paycheck, however generous, that had made him eager to do her bidding. Yeager was not like Blaine. He had ambition.

But the chill returned, and she shivered. Going to Paradise and luring Blaine back to the Rocking Chair had been an impetuous, stupid move. She should have known better.

An uneasiness began to steal over her, and she took a swift gulp of the warm wine. Surprisingly, the glass was empty again. She stared at it, wondering how she was going to handle Yeager's rage. He could be a dangerous man if he thought he was being crossed. She hadn't faced this worry directly before because she had been so certain that Blaine could handle Yeager if a conflict arose. And so convinced that Blaine could not refuse her that she hadn't faced the consequences of that refusal. She had been too busy enjoying the idea that she could make Yeager sweat and squirm. With Blaine backing her, and the men backing them both as they certainly would have, Yeager could have done nothing.

Now even this did not seem to be so certain. Or even desirable. Why had she been so anxious to replace Yeager? The wine had loosened some of her inhibitions, and the answer to that question was suddenly clearer. She was afraid of Yeager, but what she felt was . . . more than fear. Had she wanted Blaine in his place, then, because Blaine was . . . safer?

Kate was conscious suddenly of being a woman alone in a world of men, a hard, demanding world in which physical strength, endurance, and courage often ruled. It was a world in which women played an often essential but secondary, supporting role—cooking and cleaning, mending and sewing, raising vegetables and flowers and children. The house and its gardens was their province, which might extend to such domestic animals as there were. But the real work of the ranch was handled by men.

Kate hardly remembered her mother, who had died when Kate was nine. The girl had grown up in surroundings completely dominated by her father and shaped by his nature. Sean Roark had been a strong man, intolerant of weakness in himself or in others. Kate had the feeling that he had never quite forgiven her mother for being sickly, for abandoning life so early, for meekly accepting death. He had died suddenly and violently, in the only way, it seemed, that he could have given up his hold on life. She knew that he would have gone out clawing and raging, fighting for his last breath.

When it happened she had felt totally lost, demoralized. Only her own bitter anger had saved her. She had emerged from those first few days of wild grief with a determination to fight as Sean Roark would have fought, to carry on what he had begun. She wanted no soft words of consolation, no sympathy, no strong shoulder to lean on. The ranch was hers now. She would keep it. She would fight those who had been his enemies and destroy them, using the weapons which had cut him down in the full vigor of his life. Force and violence. Guns and men who knew how to use them.

For most of the time since she buried her father, Kate Roark had been too caught up in that fight and her passion to avenge his murder to allow any feelings of weakness to surface. Now the hand holding the empty wine glass trembled. She turned shakily from the window. Damn him— damn that Blaine! What kind of a man was he, anyway? She should never have gambled on her ability to sway him. When she had heard that he had hired on as Nancy Cronin's protector, she had been convinced that he was not as hellbent on his search for the man he wanted—Keatch? Was that his name?—as he pretended. She had underestimated him. . . .

Kate raised her glass as anger once more swept over her. She looked toward the far wall as if she meant to hurl this glass after the other. But the anger was a sudden gust, and in another moment it was gone, replaced by a feeling she despised, a sinking dread in the pit of her stomach.

She was afraid.

Until now she had been able to handle Clete Yeager. Sometimes it was absurdly easy. He wanted her so badly that she was able to turn that wanting against him. Cold one minute, friendly and confiding the next, switching at will from indifference to a teasing promise, she had kept Yeager rattled and uncertain—and always eager. There had even been a thrill of danger in the game. She had been careful, however, not to push him too far, sensing instinctively that the brutal violence in him might threaten even her if it were ever cut loose.

Yeager had been angry when she had had Cullom Blaine in to breakfast that first morning he came and offered him a job. This time, when he learned that she had ridden to Paradise to bring Blaine back with her, there was no telling how enraged he might be. He had sensed from the start that

Blaine might be a rival. And he would guess why she had
wanted Blaine here, working for her, doing her bidding.

Shivering, Kate Roark hugged her chest with her arms,
and in so doing became aware once more of the empty wine
glass in her hand.

The bottle on the table was not empty. After only a moment's hesitation she started toward it. Her steps were just a
little unsteady. She was unaware that she walked with exag-
gerated care, holding herself very erect, as if to assure some
unknown onlooker that she was neither drunk nor frightened.

*   *   *

The tall grandfather clock had just finished striking ten
o'clock that night when Kate heard the commotion that accompanied the return of Yeager and the other riders from
Rush City. She remained sitting in the big leather chair near
the hearth—her father's favorite chair—for she did not trust
herself to walk to the door. Let him come to her, she
thought, with an irrational resentment.

The wine bottle which she had carried from the dining
table some time before rested now on the stone hearth beside her chair. It was empty.

What do you think of that, Cullom Blaine? She giggled
suddenly, irrepressibly. Going to scold me? Send me to bed?
Spank me, like a good—

Her face was flushed with the wine, but it darkened even
more as she realized the trend of her thoughts. Her head
swam a little, and her thoughts lurched in unexpected directions, hardly coherent. But somehow she had been identi-
fying Blaine with her father. And that was absurd. She
didn't regard him in a daughterly way at all.

Several minutes had passed since the first noise of the returning riders before she heard the clomping of Clete
Yeager's boots on the porch. Her heartbeat quickened as she
waited for the knock on the door. When it came it was loud,
as angry as any mere knock could be.

"Come in!" she called nervously. "The door's not latched."

She wouldn't rise, she thought. She didn't dare. Anyway, she was in her own house. There was no reason to jump at every knock.

Clete Yeager pushed through the doorway. He gave the room a swift, sweeping glance before his gaze jerked back to her. He slammed the door behind him with what seemed needless force. When he stepped into the room so that his face caught the lamplight, she saw the dark fury in it, and for a moment panic threatened to engulf her. She fought it down, calling on her father's memory for the courage which had left her. This had been his house, his chair in which she now sat. No man would have dared to storm into this room to face him as Yeager glared at her.

"You have some explainin' to do!" he said harshly.

"Do I?" Unexpectedly her voice was quite calm, cool, and steady. "I see you've finally come back, Mr. Yeager."

"Maybe sooner than you expected," he shot back. "Or didn't things work out with Blaine the way you wanted?"

"I don't know what you mean."

"You know damned well what I mean. What did you go runnin' off to fetch him for without tellin' me?" He stalked closer to her threateningly. "Damn it, answer me!"

"I will not! I don't have to answer to you for what I do, or . . . or to ex . . . explain anything."

"Don't play the high and mighty lady with me! You've done that long enough." He stopped abruptly, staring at her closely. His gaze did not miss the creamy expanse of neck and throat and shoulders, but it took in also the glass on the hearth within reach, the empty bottle of wine, the stain splashed down the whitewashed wall in the background. "By God, you're drunk!"

"I'm not drunk!" she cried. "How dare you talk to me like this! I . . . I've had some wine, if that's what you mean." She rose from the chair, as if to assert her claim to being quite sober. But as she reached her feet she swayed, stumbled, and had to reach out to catch the back of the chair. Then, to her own horror, she felt an urge to giggle. She could not contain it. Looking up at her tall, darkly angry riding boss, she felt the bubble of laughter come. "Oh!" she murmured then. "Oh, dear." And into her eyes came a guilty, childlike pleading. She was just twenty-three years old, and for twenty-two of those years she had been sheltered, bullied, dominated, and protected by Sean Roark. Nothing had ever threatened her. Although her frequently haughty manner suggested otherwise, in truth she was younger in experience than her years. Never before in her life had she had too much to drink. She had acted recklessly this day, foolishly, courting a very real danger that now confronted her. And all she could do was giggle and, with her eyes, beseech the angry foreman for forgiveness.

"I'll be damned!" Yeager's incredulity diluted his rage. "You're drunk, all right." He stepped even closer, causing her heart to flutter wildly. "Why? What have you been up to?"

"Nothing," she retorted, her swiftly changing emotions now reaching for defiance. "I had a little wine with dinner, that's all. And that's not . . . not for you to question, Mr. Yeager. What I drink or eat is my own affair."

"With him? That makes it mine!"

She released her protective grip on the back of the leather chair, drawing herself up with great dignity. "I had good reasons. I didn't want him at Paradise, you knew that. I don't want Nancy Cronin there, and I don't want her hurt." A quick dart of memory brought new resolution to her voice. "And you've some explaining to do on that account, I think. Why did you raid Paradise last night? Did you mean to kill her, the way you did her father?"

The surprise in his eyes told her that her guess had been accurate. He *had* ordered Rocking Chair men to attack Paradise. Without consulting her.

"I told you, I never set that fire," Yeager said, still angry but now more calculating, the unbridled fury which had brought him to the house under control. "As for last night, nobody was hurt. That raid was meant to scare her off, that's all. And that don't answer why you went runnin' to fetch this Blaine. And you'll answer, Kate." He bit off her name not with intimacy but with a kind of contempt. "You've kept me shufflin' my feet outside your door long enough. That don't wash any more. I don't shuffle over drunken women."

"How dare you!"

"Oh, I dare," he said cruelly. "Are you going to tell me straight, or do I just walk out to that tool crib and put a bullet through Blaine's head?"

Her earlier fear returned with a rush. She tried but could not stop a visible trembling. "No, wait . . . you can't kill him in cold blood like that. He's no trouble to us now, don't you see that? That's why I brought him here. He's locked up, isn't he? Oh, I'd have hired him if he was willing. I thought if he'd hire on with Nancy, why shouldn't he be on our side? But when he turned me down, I wouldn't let him go. I had him locked up in that shed." The words tumbled out of her, a mingling of anxiety and truth and lies, so mixed up that she no longer was sure which was which herself. "I told you, there's more than one way to skin a cat. We can keep Blaine cooped up, or run him out of this valley, whichever. There'll be no trouble with Sheriff Toland. And Nancy Cronin won't stay at Paradise without him. Don't you see? That's why I talked Blaine into coming here."

Yeager studied her skeptically. "Yeah, maybe that's the way it happened. Maybe. How'd you talk him into it?"

A sly smile touched her lips, and her answer was eager, seeking approval. "I told him I knew where this man Keatch could be found—the one he's hunting."

Something quick and cold appeared in Yeager's eyes. "How'd you know about Keatch?"

"I . . . I don't. But I had to tell him *something*. You see that, surely."

Her explanation was plausible enough to blunt his suspicion, but he still didn't like it. He didn't like having Blaine at the Rocking Chair, and he didn't like knowing that Kate Roark had dined with him. As the hot thrust of his anger subsided, another passion began to rise, and he stared more openly at the deep cut of her bodice, which revealed the swell of her breasts provocatively. That Blaine had seen her like this rekindled his hostility toward the man.

"You had to dress like that," he said suddenly, "just to hire a man? You expect me to believe that?"

She heard a peevish jealousy in his words. They gave her a sense of triumph, and her smile broadened. A sidelong glance teased him. "What makes you think this dress was for him? You said you might be back tonight, or have you forgotten?"

The dark flush in his face and the glitter in his eyes spoke all too clearly of his long-held desire, but his tone remained harsh. "Don't lie to me—not about that."

"I'm not lying." She knew in that moment what she had to do, finally, to placate him. Laughter and promises were no longer enough.

She reached up to release the comb at the back of her head, and with it the rich dark flow of her hair, which fell over her shoulders. Her eyelids lowered slightly as she looked up at him, and a slow smile parted her lips. "Don't you think I've been waiting all this time," she murmured softly, "same as you?"

Clete Yeager reached her in one long stride and swept her into his arms.

* * *

The sky was only faintly visible when he rose from her bed. His skin looked chalk white and cold as he stood by the window, staring out thoughtfully. His body was even leaner and harder and taller than she had imagined. His strength, and the swift brutality of his loving, had frightened her and left her breathless, but now, in the early morning, she felt a languorous pleasure in her own body she had not known before.

Then he began to pull on his clothes.

"Where are you going?" Kate asked. "It's early yet."

"Early for you, maybe. But I've been waitin' a long time for this. It's late for a lot of things." His glance at her held an arrogant satisfaction, a look of smug possession that caused her to stiffen. "We've been pussy-footin' around long enough. It's time to end this so-called war, anyway. Only reason those penny-ante ranchers have stuck together this long is they haven't been hit hard enough. Well, it's time."

Alarmed, Kate sat up in bed, momentarily forgetting that she wore no gown. When a smirk touched his eyes, she drew the sheet up to her shoulders and said, "We'll have to talk this over, honey—"

"Talk's done," he said curtly. "There's been too much palaverin'. Let that Cattlemen's Association hear some buzzing around their ears. That's what they'll really listen to."

"Now wait a minute, Clete," she said more firmly. "That's not what I want. We—"

"We both know what you want," he interrupted, and the smirking satisfaction moved from his eyes to his lips. "Don't worry, you'll get plenty of that from now on. Leave it to me. I never left no woman dissatisfied yet."

She stared at him with a growing feeling of shock and dismay. My God, was this what it meant to a man when he had made love to a woman he had desired so long? That he could look on her as if she were something less than before, something he now owned and could use as he willed, like a horse broken to the saddle? And despise her a little for giving him what he had wanted?

"Don't look so worried," Yeager said, buttoning his shirt and stuffing the tail into his pants. "From now on you won't have to fret your head about anythin'. That includes Simmons and his Association. Before this day is over they'll be sorry they ever came to this valley." He paused, then added as an afterthought, "That goes for your friend down there in the tool shed."

"Rocking Chair is mine," Kate Roark cried. "I'll decide what we do with my men."

"Yeah, sure," Yeager cut her off, with an indifferent attempt to placate her that held such obvious condescension she felt quick tears rise to her eyes. "Rocking Chair is yours, no gainsayin' that. But I'll run it for both of us from now on." He was still grinning, but there was something hard and flat in his eyes that carried a different and chilling message. He approached the bed and stared down at her. Remembering the callous strength of his hands and body, Kate shivered. Yeager saw the reaction. He reached out suddenly to seize her by the shoulders, his fingers biting into the soft flesh. Kate winced, but she felt helpless, unable to pull away. "I'm runnin' things now. Learn that and we'll get along just fine. We're gonna have it all, Kate, you and me, just the way your old man had it once, just the way you've always wanted it. Old Sean, he went soft there at the last. He'd still have it all if he'd let me do things the way I wanted. Don't you make the same mistake. Don't try to tell me how or when to do things. That's over."

He released her. One hand casually caressed her shoulder, as if soothing the bruises his fingers had left. In a gentler tone he said, "Go back to sleep. I want you to look fresh and pretty again when I get back." He chuckled. "Right now you look like you had a hard night."

Still laughing softly, he turned away and scooped up the coat he had thrown to the floor in his haste earlier that night. Then he lifted his gunbelt from a chair nearby, where he had placed it with more care than he gave to anything else he wore. He was strapping on his gun when he walked out.

Kate Roark remained on the bed, feeling cold, facing the dawning realization of what she had chosen for herself. She had been afraid of Clete Yeager last night, and that fear had been behind her decision, a choice eased by all the wine she had drunk. But the terror she felt now struck far deeper. It reached into her future, exposing a life unimaginable.

What had she done to herself? And what kind of evil had she released into this valley her father had loved?

FIFTEEN

The tool shed in which Blaine was imprisoned was not sturdy enough to resist a determined effort to break out, but Rocking Chair hands took turns standing watch outside through the night, so Blaine resigned himself to a long wait. There might come a time before morning when a bored sentry would find his eyelids growing heavy.

He heard the arrival of a group of riders about two hours after the shed door had closed on him. There was a murmur of voices. One rose sharply in anger. Blaine thought he recognized Clete Yeager's tone.

So he hadn't known of Kate Roark's invitation.

Blaine put his eye to a crack between two boards. The night was overcast, the air heavy with the promise of the rain so long denied this valley. He could see little clearly, but as he stared in the direction of the main house he was able to make out a tall figure stalking toward the long porch. A heavy banging on the front door followed. When the door opened, the yellow light from within confirmed the tall man's identity. The door closed behind Yeager, leaving a deeper blackness.

Blaine waited a long time, watching the house thoughtfully, wondering how Kate would divert her jealous foreman's anger. Time gave the answer. Yeager did not come out.

After a while Blaine relaxed, settling to the dirt floor of the shed. He did not waste time railing at the woman in the house for her trickery. What mattered now was how to get out of his predicament. He doubted that even a night in

Kate Roark's bed would mollify Yeager completely. She probably expected that it would. She was young, and still had much to learn about men of Yeager's stamp.

He heard the midnight change of sentries, after which he slept himself. In the small hours of darkness, awake again, he heard the man on watch begin to snore and whistle, his breathing deep and regular. Carefully, using the handle of a shovel, Blaine tried to pry out a large knot in one of the boards of the door. It popped out unexpectedly, landing with a light clatter on something hard on the ground outside the shed.

The sentry, a lighter sleeper than his breathing had suggested, jumped awake.

He inspected the big knothole and chuckled. "Hell, if'n you can wriggle out of a hole that size, I'd likely mistaken you for a rattlesnake. I'd have to stomp you to a pancake and cut off your rattles for a trophy."

Blaine contemplated his chances of ramming the shovel handle through the hole fast enough and accurately enough to disable the sentry without arousing others. The chances seemed to be on the narrow side of slim. He said, "Sorry to wake you."

The sentry chuckled appreciatively.

Moments later he was resting with his back against the nearby barn—wide awake and out of reach.

Blaine was dozing when he heard the sounds of a number of men cutting their horses from the corral, saddling up and assembling. He put his eye to the knothole. Mists hugged the ground in the feeble light, obscuring his view of horses and riders.

The sound of a door closing drew his gaze toward the house. Yeager appeared, a dim figure that grew taller as the man tramped across the yard. He detoured abruptly on a line that brought him straight toward the tool shed.

"I'd like to take time for you now, Blaine," he said. "But

you're not important enough. I'll leave you to sweat it out.
When I get back, you'll wish I'd done it quicker."

Blaine was content to remain silent, guessing that any
angry protest would simply add to the gunman's satisfaction
in having him caged.

Yeager started to swing away, stopped, and turned back.
He approached the shed slowly. "Another thing, Blaine.
That hair-trigger man you've been askin' about. I'll be seein'
Keatch this morning. You got any message you want me to
deliver?"

Blaine's mouth went dry, and his heart hammered. That
was the way it always was when he got close to one of
Samantha's killers. That would never change.

When he said nothing, Yeager chuckled. "Might be he'll
be interested in knowing you're swimmin' in a barrel,
Blaine. We could all enjoy some target practice."

He stalked off toward the corral, joining the handful of
waiting riders. They rode out immediately into the gray
mist, quickly lost to sight beyond the barn. A heavy silence
closed in behind them.

Blaine choked back the anger Yeager had aroused by his
mention of Ned Keatch. He tried to think past it. What was
Yeager up to? Where was he going? What was important
enough to cause him to leave the pleasure of Kate Roark's
arms so early? With only three or four men beside him, he
could hardly be planning a big raid. What, then?

And where did Keatch fit in?

Frowning, Blaine slumped back onto the cold floor. He
didn't like it. Whatever had taken Yeager off at this hour
had to be important. He seemed to have been close to most
of the bad trouble that had struck the ranchers in Antelope
Valley this past year—on either side. It was a good bet that
someone was going to run into unexpected trouble again.

The gray predawn light was beginning to penetrate the
interior of the crib, and Blaine began a more thorough
search of its contents than he had been able to make in total

darkness. There were shovels, a post hole digger, some old harness, a coil of wire, a tomato tin filled with nails. Nothing that looked very promising.

By the time he had completed his search and settled down once more, the morning had begun to lighten. There would be no sun visible this day. A gray gloom hung over the land, with dark clouds stretching from the peaks of the Towers all the way to the eastern horizon. There was a brisk wind, too, flattening the dry grass and sending ragged puffs of dust scurrying across the yard.

He would have to take his chances, Blaine thought. Put a heel into that door hard enough to split it away from the lock. Then move fast enough to reach the sentinel on duty before he could blink the dust out of his eyes. A long gamble, but the only one left. And it had to be done before the whole Rocking Chair crew was up and about, which wouldn't be long now.

How long since Yeager had ridden out? Upward of an hour, Blaine reckoned. No way to measure time accurately in this tiny shack, cut off from night or morning sky. During that hour Blaine's feeling that this day promised real trouble had been steadily heightening. Yeager had had every reason to linger late in a warm bed this morning. That he hadn't done so was ominous.

Blaine picked up a long-handled shovel to use as a weapon. He was turning toward the door when he heard footsteps. A voice called out cheerfully, "That spine of yours must be plumb wore out, Spud, curled up that way. Maybe a spell in your bunk will straighten it out."

Blaine's hope sagged. He recognized the voice as belonging to Walden, and any confidence he had about breaking out vanished. Walden was not a careless man. He was also fresh and wide awake, not a tired sentry dreaming of his bunk.

"What about the prisoner?"

"I'll take care of him. I just come from the house, as you

coulda seen if you was awake. Miss Roark wants to see him again."

There was a momentary pause before the sentry said, "What's goin' on, Walden?"

"Nobody tells me much," Walden answered.

"You know more'n you let on. Hell, you know better'n anybody else we ain't gettin' much work done with all this chasin' around. That west herd's drifted so far it's gonna raise hell findin' the strays and drivin' 'em back to the home range. We don't do it soon, by spring what's left of 'em will be clear over in Montana."

It was a working cowboy's complaint, and in it Blaine also heard an exasperation with the valley's quarrels that had erupted into violence. He wondered how many of the Rocking Chair's crew felt the same. Most of those who hadn't been hired lately for their quick guns alone, he judged.

His attention shifted to Walden's puzzling comment about Kate Roark. Why would she be sending for him now? Somehow, after what had happened this night, the invitation seemed unlikely.

"Maybe things'll change soon," Walden said to the sentry.

"Yeah, and maybe there's five aces in the deck," Spud grumbled.

"Go get some sleep."

Blaine heard the sentry's weary footsteps plod out of earshot. Only then did a key grind in the padlock and pop it open. The door creaked open on the gray pallor of the morning.

Walden beckoned him out of the shed.

"You servin' breakfast this morning, Walden?" Blaine drawled.

The bearded cowpuncher smiled thinly—acknowledgment enough for a poor joke at this hour, Blaine thought. Then he noticed that Walden did not have his gun in his hand, and that he seemed to be paying more attention to the quiet bunkhouse than to his prisoner. "If I was you, I wouldn't stop for breakfast this side of Kansas." Walden's gaze flicked back to him. "But I don't reckon that's what you'll do."

"What's up?" Blaine asked alertly. "I heard you say Miss Roark wanted to see me."

"Not this mornin'," Walden said. "I don't reckon she'd want to look you in the eye. But she don't want to see you pushin' up daisies neither on her account, which is what'll happen if you're still here when Yeager gets back."

"She told you to cut me loose?"

"Stop askin' questions, Blaine. Your horse is waitin' on the morning side of the barn."

"What's Yeager going to say when he gets back and finds he's got an empty barrel?"

Walden shrugged. "Could be that latch'll be broke loose when he looks at it. And bein' the heller you are, I reckon you might've had a hide-out gun tucked up your sleeve, so you got the jump on me."

"He won't like it."

"Maybe my ears'll burn, but it won't be the first time."

Blaine looked at him, hesitating. But no cowhand expected vocal gratitude for a favor, even if it saved your hide from being nailed to a fence. Walden would only be made uncomfortable if Blaine thanked him. In any event, the idea hadn't been his.

"I reckon Kate made a mistake last night," he said quietly. "Do you suppose she knows it this morning?"

"Ain't for me to say," Walden snapped back. He and most of the other hands would have seen the same thing Blaine saw, and Walden was troubled by it.

Blaine nodded then, accepting his luck. Whether it had come from a momentary whim or a severe attack of remorse hardly mattered.

But as he started to turn away, something stopped him. It didn't seem enough simply to take his luck and run, leaving Kate Roark to the misery she had freely chosen. She had lied to him, tricked him into a trap, but he still had the feeling that she was more impetuous than evil. Vain, perhaps. Proud and bitter, certainly. But at the same time generous, passionate, loyal. Her drive for revenge had been born out of love and loyalty for her dead father. She deserved better than Clete Yeager's usage of her.

She had been looking in the wrong direction for Sean Roark's real enemies, Blaine thought. He glanced at Walden. "When Roark was shot down," he said, "did anything about it ever strike you as unlikely?"

Walden frowned. "Only one thing. That he never cleared leather."

"And he wasn't shot in the back?"

"No. What are you gettin' at, Blaine?"

"It struck me as strange that a man like Roark would have let himself be taken so easily by a stranger. From all I've heard of him, he wasn't that careless. It bothered Sheriff Toland, too, that Roark was alone."

"He sent Yeager back ahead—" Walden broke off. In the silence that followed Blaine watched the idea take hold.

"Yeager found him, I reckon."

"That's right, but . . . hell, Collins lit out!"

"Uh-huh. Sometimes a man will run scared when he knows a thing looks bad for him, even if he didn't do it. Suppose you were Collins and you saw Yeager draw on his own boss, and then turn his gun on you and tell you to high tail it, because that shooting was gonna be blamed on you. What the hell would you do?"

"I'd run," Walden admitted. "But it won't wash, Blaine. Yeager had nothin' to gain by it. Roark hired him! He had no reason to kill him."

"He had one I know of," Blaine answered quietly. "Maybe there were others, but . . . would Roark have let a gunslinger near his daughter?"

The sudden shift in Walden's eyes told him the man was no longer automatically rejecting his argument. A hard, bitter anger tightened Walden's mouth. "No, he wouldn't. Never."

"Were you along when Collins was treed?"

"I was there. Hell, I never thought about him runnin' if he didn't do it."

"Did Collins have a chance to say anything?"

"No, he was yellin' something, and Yeager . . ." Walden was silent again, remembering how it had happened.

"Yeager made sure he never had a chance to speak out for himself. That the way it happened?"

"That's about it. But this is all guesswork, Blaine. There's no way to back it up."

"Except that Sean Roark was sittin' easy in the saddle, his gun in its holster, when somebody blew him down. Do you really think that could have happened if the man in front of him was a hired gun workin' for the Association?"

"I dunno. . . ." Walden shook his head, obviously disturbed by Blaine's suggestion but still not convinced. He'd work it out, Blaine thought, now that the notion had been planted.

"It's worth thinkin' about," Blaine said. "Might even be something Kate Roark hasn't ever suspected." He paused. "She's dug herself a hole, Walden. No reason she has to stay in it. Maybe she won't even want to."

He started toward the barn. Walden took a step after him. "You're goin' after him with one hand to use?"

"Better that than wait for him to come to me."

"You'll find your rifle where it belongs. And your Colt's inside the saddlebag."

Blaine nodded. "See you, then."

"I doubt it," Walden answered. "But if it was to happen, I can't say I'd be surprised."

* * *

The wide cattle trail dipped across a gully. At the bottom Clete Yeager parted company with the three other Rocking

Chair riders. They had their instructions. All three were dead-eyed, hard-bitten men who didn't ask questions if the pay was right. They were in a class with Keatch, he thought, and he had hand-picked them.

Yeager watched them climb out of the gully. Then he turned left along the dry bottom.

An hour later he slanted along a trail that followed a canyon. Its mouth opened out onto the flats near the southwest corner of the valley.

Yeager studied the terrain as he rode on. There was dry brush and some grass on the rocky hills to the west, but the wind—strong this morning—was coming down off the hills. With that wind to carry it, a fire would race across the valley like a stampede, and just as unstoppable.

He pulled up when he reckoned that he was due east of the headquarters of the Paradise. Even if the fire never got that far, or took off in another direction, it would blacken the Paradise's valley range. Although the grass crop had been poor after two dry summers, what there was had been sun-cured on the stem. It would burn like kindling. There would be little left for any cattle to feed on this winter. Without grass, and with Blaine out of the picture, the Cronin woman would be finished once and for all.

Of course, Rocking Chair cattle would also be denied this graze for a long time—a burned-off range recovered slowly. But it would be worth the price. The members of the Cattlemen's Association would read the message. Yeager didn't believe there was all that much fight in them. Not if you started to hit them hard enough.

Dismounting, he unrolled a pack he had brought with him. It included a couple of gunny sacks, some wire, rope, and a can of kerosene. He tied the tops of the sacks together with wire, using about ten feet of the wire to extend out from the sacks. He attached the free end of the wire to the rope, which he then secured to his saddlehorn.

When this was ready, he poured the kerosene over the

gunny sacks. Stepping back, he struck a match and tossed it toward the saturated sacks. They burst into flame. The explosion was sharper than he had expected, and he jumped back in alarm. But the fiery ball subsided quickly, and in an instant the grass around the sacks began to burn.

Grinning, Yeager stepped into the saddle. He proceeded north across the valley, dragging the burning torch behind him through the dry grass, leaving behind a trail of fire. The wire attached to the gunny sacks turned hot and black, but it wouldn't burn, and the flames did not reach the length of rope between Yeager and the fire.

He had covered more than a hundred yards before the gunny sacks began to burn out. He freed the rope, dropped it, and cantered away.

From a ridge to the west he watched the line of fire move eastward across the valley floor, fanned by the steady wind, crackling and spitting sparks, slowly building to a solid wall of flames and gathering speed as it went.

A gust of damp, heavy air caused Yeager to glance skyward, scowling. There was rain in the black clouds overhead. The smell of it was in the wind. But no matter, he thought. It wouldn't come in time.

SIXTEEN

Cullom Blaine rode across the damp meadow east of the Rocking Chair's headquarters at a gallop, putting sudden distance between himself and the early risers among the ranch hands who might come looking for him. Some of them might be friendlier to Clete Yeager than Walden was, and less loyal to the woman who was their real boss. Only when the house and its outbuildings were out of sight did Blaine slow the buckskin's pace. The horse was fresh and eager, and the morning was cool under its cloudy sky, but Blaine was no longer in a hurry. He knew the heavy dew on the grass would hold sign for a while, and it didn't take long to find the tracks left by Yeager and three other riders.

They were, he judged, about an hour ahead of him.

The tracks took him northeast, in the general direction of Rush City, but they vanished when they merged into a broad cattle trail. Disappointed, Blaine followed the wide trail, wondering what Yeager could be up to in town.

He had been on the trail about a half hour when it dipped across a gully and, a quarter mile beyond the dip, forked in two directions. The main trail continued northeast. The left fork pointed north. Blaine followed it only a short distance before he was able to make out the fresh tracks. He wondered whose spread lay in this direction, and regretted not asking more questions about the various small ranchers who belonged to the Cattlemen's Association.

The tracks crossed a grassy patch, and Blaine stopped short, staring at the ground.

There were only three sets of tracks.

He knew instantly that the one who had cut loose from the others had to be Yeager. But where? How far back? Had he taken the main fork toward town, or left the trail at some other place Blaine had missed?

More impatient now, Blaine doubled back. He had to choose one side of the trail or the other, and his first choice was to swing a hundred yards to the west, heading back toward the Rocking Chair on a line that paralleled the road he had followed in Yeager's wake. He came to the gully he had crossed before, dropped to the bottom, and he scanned it in both directions. It was a dry wash with a gravel floor, but here and there some occasional runoff had left sand instead of gravel. He saw the fresh cut of a hoof in sand almost immediately.

The sign pointed west, and Blaine followed it eagerly. The gully soon opened out, and the tracks climbed onto a broad table. From there Blaine had no trouble tracking. Apparently Yeager did not expect anyone to be following him so soon, and he had made no attempt to hide his trail.

It was full daylight, and the sun was slanting through a break in the dark clouds far off to the east, lighting up the whole horizon with a strange brilliance, when he saw the thin cloud of smoke off to the north.

Blaine frowned uneasily. That smoke looked thin, but it was a long way off. There was a lot more of it than showed. And it meant only one thing: fire.

Fire was a personal thing to Cullom Blaine, an evil thing. It made his flesh crawl, and it brought a chill to the back of his neck that seemed to strike through to his brain.

He turned toward higher ground, reluctantly abandoning Yeager's trail for the moment.

Before he reached the rim he sought, he was able to make out the red stain on the bottoms of the black clouds riding above the smoke, a reflection of the flames below, and he urged his horse into a run.

From a ledge of rimrock above the valley floor Blaine had

his first clear view of the fire. It was still miles away, burning across the grassy floor, moving steadily to the east. Even at this distance it was awesome and terrible, for Blaine had known the fury of a prairie fire long before the awful morning when his own home burned to the ground.

He turned his face into the wind. It was blowing due east. Strongly. It would carry that wall of flame across the valley with the speed of a locomotive under full steam.

And it was heading straight toward the Paradise.

There was a long moment when Blaine considered his choice. Clete Yeager's tracks—he was certain in his mind that the lone rider had to be Yeager—were heading westward. They might even swing behind that fire. They were also carrying Yeager to a meeting with Ned Keatch.

There had been no reason for Yeager to lie, not when he was talking to a man locked up and under guard. He was not worrying about anyone trailing him, and there seemed a good chance that he would continue to be careless. Careless enough to lead Blaine straight to Keatch.

But the fire pulled him in another direction. It had to be stopped. It wouldn't touch him—he had nothing now that fire could harm—and there would surely be others seeing this smoke, giving the alarm, racing to help. But he thought about Nancy Cronin, alone at Paradise with fire racing down on her, and knew that he could not take the risk.

Blaine had thought that nothing could divert him from one of Samantha's killers once he had got the scent and was closing in. Now he learned, with a sting of surprise, that he had changed a little in these long months of hunting, months that had taken him far from home, far from the knoll where Samantha and their unborn child were buried. He had begun to notice other things, even to begin to care about them. Even if it meant letting Keatch get away, he couldn't leave Nancy alone to face that red fury.

Blaine set off on a lope toward the Paradise range. Fire could race at dangerous speeds when the wind caught it, but it was also hungry, and it would slow at times to consume the grass and brush before it moved on. There was a good chance that he could get ahead of it. It meant a long, punishing ride for Randy, which Blaine didn't like. A cowman's working horse, durable and intelligent, Randy was adapted more to short bursts of speed than the long-distance running that suited a cavalry horse or an Indian pony. Blaine was glad of the cloud cover that made the morning cooler. Heat could be the killer on a hard run.

The closer he came to Paradise, the higher the bank of smoke climbed off to his left, until it merged into the tumbling darkness of the storm clouds and made the whole western horizon a blending grayness, the Towers completely hidden from view. By the time he reached the wagon road that circled south of Paradise, the air was filled with ashes whirling like black snow, like the first flakes of an approaching storm.

No smoke curled from the bunkhouse stack. Scanning the area hurriedly as he rode up, Blaine observed no sign of life. Even the corral was empty.

Reining in, Blaine spilled to the ground and hit the bunkhouse door on the run. The shack was empty. Emerging, he was struck by a feeling of desolation about the place, the same air of abandonment it had had when he first came to it from town with Nancy Cronin. But at that time it had stood empty for several months. Less than twenty-four hours ago she had been here, the stove had been hot, the string of horses had been either in the corral or in the grazing meadow.

Had she gone back to town, then? Given up because he had left her? Blaine scowled at the thought. He didn't believe it. She wouldn't have quit so soon.

No, it was the cloud cover, along with the drifting smoke and ashes, which had brought this sudden gloom to the Paradise. Nancy must have spied the smoke to the west. She would have wanted to get her horses clear of it, certainly.

This seemed the only hopeful explanation of her absence among several possibilities, and Blaine latched onto it. He saw no morning tracks around the yard to suggest that—

A rider burst over the rise to the east. A lone rider. Blaine stepped out to watch him approach. He veered away from the trail and cut straight across the open plain. He lathered down the last slope at full gallop, and Blaine didn't recognize him until he was close. It was Simmons.

Simmons barreled across the yard, skidding up a cloud of dust as he pulled up hard. His sturdy mare's forelegs bounced. Simmons threw a wild glance around the yard before he called out sharply. "Where's Nancy?"

"Not here," Blaine said. "I just got back."

"You left her alone again?"

Blaine ignored the hostile question. "My guess is she drove her horses off, maybe took them to the other side of the river and down east, away from the fire."

Simmons stared at him, but he wasted no time in unnecessary questions or recriminations. Instead he said, "Any chance of stopping that fire before it gets here?"

"It'll take what's left of this place if we don't."

"How about a backfire?"

"Won't work. Nothin' to back it up against." A backfire needed a natural barrier to work effectively against a fire like this one, a wide trail the fire couldn't jump, or an arroyo or other break. "Wait a minute—that wash to the south, we might stop it there." His thoughts raced ahead, measuring the width of the draw, the wagon trail that crossed it and then swung along the west side of the bank. There might be a chance. "We've got to turn it. Keep it away from those hills and swing it south toward that draw."

Simmons looked dubious. "There's help coming. I saw dust behind me."

"No time to wait. They can work the draw if they get here quick enough. But we've got to turn it."

"You have an idea how we'll do that, just the two of us?"

Blaine's gaze flicked toward the hills behind the shell of the old house. He had seen a few steers milling around there when he arrived. One ran down the hillside now, followed incongruously by a bounding antelope. "We'll cut out one of those beeves," he said tersely. "And make a drag."

He was vaulting into the saddle before he finished speaking. Simmons followed him past the ruins of the house and they cantered up the hillside. The cattle, already spooked by the fire, ran from them. The steer Blaine picked out tried to get away, but the buckskin quickly headed it off and turned it back. By then Simmons was swinging to the other side of the critter. Together the two men herded the frightened steer down the hillside and drove it toward the open.

When they came around the corner of the hill, the full fury of the fire burst upon them. It was closer than Blaine had thought, and the earlier spray of black flakes and smoke had given way to a hail of cinders and flying sparks. The steer bolted in panic, but Simmons was ready for it. His rope whistled as it flew out to drop over the horns.

The fear-crazed animal fought the rope. Simmons' horse dug in and wheeled, throwing the steer in a wide circle that carried it toward Blaine. He had his Winchester out. Swinging clear of the kicking, bawling critter, he put a bullet into its neck. It dropped quickly, and Blaine killed it with a second, more carefully placed shot.

"You'll have to do the cutting," he told Simmons. "My hand isn't up to it."

Simmons swung down from his horse, but then he hesitated, uncertainty showing.

"It's a wet drag," Blaine explained. "Skin one side. Cut around the legs and up the belly, and peel the hide back. Let it flap loose. The hide will help to put out some of the sparks we don't smother."

Once he had grasped the idea of what was wanted, Sim-

mons set to work quickly and efficiently, stripping the hide
from one side of the dead steer. At Blaine's suggestion he
cut off the head, since the horns would otherwise have inter-
fered with the drag. When he finished his hasty work Simmons was sweating, and the smell of raw meat and blood
mingled sharply with the heavy, stinging smoke that blew
around them.

Working under Blaine's directions, the two men looped
their ropes over front and hind legs of the carcass. They
were thus able to drag the dead animal crosswise, creating a
heavy drag along the ground, wet side down.

The fire was moving swiftly toward them. Because it was
being driven eastward by the wind, it had been contained
by the wagon trail that laced away from the hills to the
west, following the line of the nearby stream. But that trail
swung south just about where Blaine and Simmons were
standing, and there was no doubt that the fire would jump
the trail unless it could be diverted to the south, where the
dry wash presented a more formidable barrier.

A wall of smoke rose above the line of the fire, red at the
bottom, then pink, then black as it climbed higher. The
wind was hot and strong, blowing in sudden, hammering
gusts that whirled smoke and sparks this way and that. Here
and there a burning cow chip was picked up and bowled
along the ground. Tumbleweeds and other brush shot up
into the air like fiery cannon balls, some of them carrying
over great distances, igniting new fires where they landed
ahead of the main blaze.

"Over there!" Blaine shouted above the crackling and
popping of flames. "We'll have to work from the side."

They moved away from the front of the fire, which was
now hot enough to blister their hands and faces. They
dragged the carcass between them. Swinging into position
near the bottom of the low hill they were trying to protect,
Blaine nodded at Simmons. He took the inside path himself,
walking over the blackened turf on the inward side of the

fire line, with Simmons on the outside, the heavy carcass pulled over the flames between them.

At this edge of the fire the flames were not as high and fierce, but the ground still smoked. Within minutes the buckskin was prancing gingerly, his hoofs baked by the hot ground with its coating of ashes. Soot kicked up by his heels covered both the horse and Blaine, so they were soon blackened from head to foot.

When he sensed that Randy needed relief, Blaine switched ropes and positions with Simmons, who took the inward side of the drag. Their pace was agonizingly slow, and Blaine had a feeling that the effort was pitifully small against a blaze of this size. Still, it was not long before they had covered the length of the loop of the wagon trail between the fire and the hillside behind them. Looking back, Blaine saw that the fire was effectively extinguished along the path of the drag. The flames, taking the easier path, were moving more rapidly toward the southeast.

Wearily the two men retraced their ground, pulling the charred carcass over the scorched earth to make a wider gap for the fire to jump. They were near the end of the line when Blaine's rope burned through, and he pulled away from the fire line.

By then the drag had done most of what it could accomplish. The buckskin had had enough, and Blaine wasn't sure which one of them was more nearly finished. Simmons pulled away from the edge of the fire to join him. They stared at each other with red eyes, exhausted, black with soot, hair singed and lungs aching.

A signal from Simmons turned Blaine around. Another rider had materialized out of the smoke on the far side of the draw. The rider stood there a moment, taking in the scene, then swung away and disappeared. A moment later Nancy Cronin galloped around the curve of the hill behind them.

The young woman stared at the two soot-covered men.

Her mouth opened as she looked at Simmons, but she jerked her gaze back to Blaine before she spoke. "So you came back," she said.

"Be glad he did," Brad Simmons said. "Turning the fire like that was his idea. I didn't think we could do it, but damned if we didn't."

"We didn't stop it," Blaine said wearily, looking off toward the flames that ate steadily toward the draw. "It'll jump that wash. Wind's too high. All we did was keep it away from these hills and the buildings on the other side."

"You did more than that," Nancy Cronin said. "And now you've got help coming. Haven't you looked behind you yet?"

"Who—?" The question died as Blaine swung around. He felt a rush of elation.

He had heard no rumble of warning, seen no lightning, perhaps because he had been so intent on fighting the fire. Now, marching across the valley toward them like some invincible army, came the rain. The clouds had opened, releasing the long-promised and long-delayed downpour over the smoking valley.

Blaine found himself grinning broadly as the first pelting drops reached him. He lifted his face to the rain. He heard Brad Simmons' joyous yip and saw his hat fly high into the air. Then a heavy sheet of rain arrived, drenching him instantly.

The fire, already turned and slowed at the edge of the draw, would soon be out.

SEVENTEEN

For ten minutes the rain thundered down in an all-out cloudburst. Then, almost as suddenly as it had come, the storm moved on, leaving behind only a fine, soft mist of rain. Clouds still tumbled over most of the valley, but to the west, at the far end, the wet hills sparkled in sunlight.

Blaine, Simmons, and Nancy Cronin had temporarily taken refuge in the shelter of the bunkhouse. The two men were a sorry-looking pair, but their drenching had at least served to wash away most of the coating of soot and ashes. While they waited out the storm, Nancy learned of Blaine's return shortly ahead of Simmons, who admitted soberly that he had not known of the fire until he was near the Paradise. He had been coming over for another talk with Nancy. He didn't want her to stay here, regardless of Blaine's presence.

Staring out at the thinning rain, Simmons said, "It's the worst kind of luck, Nancy, losing all that graze, but I doubt you lost many beeves. Most of them had time to get to the other side of the river safe, and the fire didn't jump it. It might have gone worse," he added, "if Blaine hadn't been here."

"And you," she reminded him.

Simmons grinned with boyish pleasure. He looked as if he wanted to say more, but he glanced at Blaine and hesitated. Blaine wondered what else he had intended to say to Nancy when he set out for Paradise that morning.

In the silence Blaine said, "There was no luck about it, good or bad."

"What do you mean?" Simmons asked, startled.

"That fire didn't start by itself. There might have been some lightning off that way this morning, but I don't think that started it."

"What are you tryin' to say?" Simmons was alert now, shedding his fatigue.

"I think that fire was set. And I've a pretty fair idea who did it."

While Simmons stared at him, Blaine was aware also of the question in Nancy Cronin's eyes. Until now she had not asked what had happened with Kate Roark at the Rocking Chair.

"Yeager?" Simmons snapped.

"That's right."

"I don't doubt it, but what makes you so sure?"

"I was trackin' him this morning when I saw the fire smoke."

There was a brief, taut silence. Then Simmons said, "Mind tellin' us how that come about?"

Blaine glanced at Nancy Cronin, remembering how accurately she had warned him of what he was getting into. Briefly he recounted his trip to the Rocking Chair the previous day with Kate Roark, riding over Simmons' exclamation of surprise at Kate's visit to Paradise. He told of her job offer and his refusal, resulting in his being clapped into the tool shed under guard. When he concluded with the manner of his release that morning, he realized that, in spite of his reticence in the narrative, it had become clear to both Nancy and Simmons that something had occurred between Kate and Clete Yeager during the night. But instead of the blame he had half expected to read in Nancy's eyes, he found only sadness.

"Poor Kate," she said softly.

"Poor Kate, hell!" Simmons said. "She's made her own bed . . ." He left the comment unfinished.

"You didn't always feel that way," Nancy retorted, moved

to defend the other woman out of sympathy or remembered friendship or simple femininity.

"That was a long time ago, Nancy. Don't you realize that?"

There was an awkward silence then. Blaine had the feeling that something was finally coming into the open between Nancy and Simmons that had been a long time surfacing.

But Simmons' anger diverted him. He slammed a fist into his palm. "By God, this time Yeager's gone too far! It means only one thing. He's tired of nibbling around the edges. He wants the whole hog. He means to smoke us all out of this valley, one way or another."

"We don't know that for sure," Nancy Cronin said quickly, more out of sudden anxiety than conviction.

"How much plainer does it have to be?" Simmons demanded angrily. "He wants a fight. Well, that's just what he's gonna get. This time he'll find us ready for him."

"What . . . what are you going to do?"

"What I should have done a long time ago. I'm roundin' up the rest of the Association's hands, every man who can ride and shoot, and takin' the fight to Yeager!"

"You can't start a shooting war! It'll mean too much killing . . . on both sides."

"I won't be the one who's started it. Anyway, what else is there to do? We can't just sit back and wait for him to burn us all out." He broke off to stare at her. "Come with me, Nancy. You shouldn't be here like this. It wasn't safe before, and it won't be now."

"I belong here," she answered stiffly.

"No, you don't, you belong with me." He stopped, as if surprised by his own words. Nancy stared at him as if she had been struck. Simmons went on more quietly, "That's something else I should have said a long time ago."

"Oh, Brad," she whispered.

"Come with me. You can stay at my place—"

"No," she said. "This isn't the time. I . . . I'll be here when you come back." A bitterness trembled in her voice. His words were what she had longed to hear for as many years as she could remember. Now they had come, but at the wrong time. They were like a soldier's proposal on the eve of going off to battle. She turned away in tears.

Simmons took her by the shoulders. "Don't worry," he said gently. "I will be back. And when I come, you won't be bothered by Yeager and his crew of cutthroats any more."

She said nothing, not trusting herself to speak. Simmons shot a glance at Blaine then, as if questioning him. When Blaine made no comment, Simmons nodded curtly, accepting his apparent decision. Blaine had no part in the valley's fight, not when it came down to gunplay.

Simmons pushed open the door and stepped out into the light drizzle. He stalked across the muddy ground to his horse, which was tethered by the corral. Nancy Cronin ran out after him, and Blaine stepped from the shack to watch them.

Nancy stopped helplessly in the middle of the yard. Simmons, his face tight and determined, gave her a last look. Then he loped away, mud flying from his mare's hoofs.

They watched him until he topped the rise and dropped out of sight. Slowly Nancy Cronin moved back to the bunkhouse and stopped at Blaine's side. "Are you leaving, too?" she asked after a moment.

"Yes, I have unfinished business."

She nodded, as if he had said only what she expected. "I'm grateful for what you've done. I have no right to ask any more."

Whatever Blaine might have replied would not be known, for at that instant they heard the crack of a rifle.

* * *

Blaine swore softly to himself as he ran toward his buckskin horse. He was remembering suddenly that

Simmons had mentioned dust behind him—but no help had materialized to fight the fire. Tied in with this rifle fire, the dust told a story. Someone had been behind Simmons, someone unwilling to reveal himself. And Blaine remembered Simmons' habit of taking off on his own, something that had seemed foolhardy for the leader of the Cattlemen's Association.

He thought of the three men who had set off with Yeager that morning.

A second shot cracked before Blaine reached the rise to the east. He burst recklessly over the hump on the run, his Winchester unsheathed and gripped in his good left hand, guiding Randy more with his knees than the reins he could only hold loosely.

Simmons was down. His mare had skittered off to the right after her rider fell. One other rider was visible, approaching Simmons across the open. He pulled up sharply as Blaine appeared, hesitated, then wheeled about and galloped away.

He was joined by two other riders at the far end of the open stretch of prairie. Blaine saw a puff of smoke and in an instant heard the crack of a rifle shot, but the shot had been a hasty, token one. The trio of riders quickly disappeared behind another roll in the plain. Blaine's fleeting wonder at the alacrity of their retreat dissipated when he heard Nancy Cronin's horse behind him. The attackers couldn't have been sure who she was or how many more were coming. They had caught Simmons alone, and they had hoped to finish him off quickly. They weren't so eager for an all-out fight against more or less equal odds.

Three riders, Blaine thought again. It was too much of a coincidence for him to doubt that they had been carrying out Yeager's orders.

Simmons hadn't moved, but as Blaine splashed up to him —he had fallen in a hollow where the sudden rain had collected—he tried to struggle up. His six-gun was in his hand, and his eyes were wild.

He didn't get a chance to fire by mistake. As Blaine veered aside and shouted, Simmons collapsed. This time he lay still.

Nancy Cronin raced up as Blaine bent over the fallen man. The bullet which had knocked Simmons out of the saddle had struck him high on the left shoulder. A sniper with a rifle, shooting at a target on horseback, tended to aim high, trying to hit the largest part of the torso, unless he was satisfied to bring down the rider's horse. If the bullet had hit bone, smashing the shoulder, the damage would be something Simmons would live with for a long time. But he would live. There was a chance, however, Blaine thought, that the bullet had only torn flesh as it passed through—a wound more painful than crippling.

Nancy Cronin was sobbing as she ran toward Simmons. Blaine rose to catch her by the shoulders, holding her back for a moment. "It's all right, he's gonna be all right."

"But his shoulder—!"

"The bullet hit high. He's hurt, but he'll live. And lucky for that. I should have guessed this might happen—that Yeager would try to cut Simmons down first. Even the fire might have been meant to draw him—"

"Lucky! How can you say that?" she cried angrily. "Let me by . . . please, Mr. Blaine!"

He stepped back, seeing that she was already calmer, panic blunted by the delaying action of his words. She knelt beside Simmons, who was unconscious. Blaine had seen shock and pain do that before, and he had an idea that Simmons would soon come out of it. Better to get him back to the bunkhouse before then. It would be a painful trip if he were awake.

Nancy Cronin cradled Simmons' head in her arms. She was kneeling in mud and water, oblivious of them, tears streaming down her cheeks. When Blaine spoke to her, she stared at him blankly. "Those men may be back," he said more sharply. "We can't stay here. And we can't do him any good here."

It took a moment for the good sense of what he said to cut through her anguish. Then she was blinking back the tears, visibly pulling herself together, and she nodded jerkily. "Tell me what to do, Mr. Blaine."

* * *

They carried Simmons back to the bunkhouse draped across his saddle. He was awake and groaning by the time they made it, and he even made an effort to stay on his feet as Blaine half carried him inside. He passed out again when they stretched him out on Nancy Cronin's bed.

Nancy Cronin took over then with a firmness that brought a faint smile to Blaine's lips. He watched her strip the shirt away from Simmons' shoulder and begin to try to stop the bleeding. After a moment he stepped outside, carrying his rifle, wondering if the three bushwhackers would have the nerve to make another try.

There was no sign of them. When several minutes passed, Blaine concluded that they must have realized they had to hit fast and run. The fire smoke would have been seen a long way off, and it would bring help soon, even though it was no longer needed to fight the fire.

When Nancy Cronin joined him outside after a while, she was pale and shaken, but Blaine thought there was also something like relief in her eyes. He wondered if she had realized that Simmons had indeed been lucky—and that he was now out of the valley's war for a long time to come.

There was no bullet, she said. And as nearly as she could tell, the shoulder had not been smashed. Simmons was resting now, but he would need a doctor. All too often the infection that followed a bullet wound could be more dangerous than the initial damage.

"You'll have help soon enough," Blaine said. "That smoke

will bring someone—and there's a good man with wounds over at Tucker's place, if you can't get him to a doctor in a hurry."

Fresh alarm sprang to her eyes as she realized the implication of his words. "Mr. Blaine, there were three of those men! You can't be going after them."

"Not them," he said quietly.

She stared at him for a long moment. "Yeager!"

"Yes, him . . . and maybe someone else."

She started to speak, but the protest died on her lips. It would do no good to point out that his gun hand was still almost useless, and that Yeager had already gunned down a string of healthy men. No words would stop him. Nor anything else at all.

EIGHTEEN

Cullom Blaine rode west across the burned-out end of the valley. It was an unreal world. Smoke still rose from the blackened grasses like steam. The wind close to the land blew hot and smelled of ashes and death. Here and there a cow chip smoldered or a black-coated mesquite bush sent up blue wisps of smoke. He saw an occasional carcass of a calf trapped in a ravine or of an old cow that had been too slow to escape, but there had been fortunately little loss of life in the fire. Still, it was like a land of the dead. All was silent. There was no movement of any kind. Blaine remembered an old cowman's phrase for such a fire-blasted place: "Hell without the company."

The desolation brought a steady anger, making him aware of a new ambivalence in his feelings. He had come to this valley to find Keatch, nothing else. That purpose still burned in him as hot as ever. But this morning he had allowed himself to be diverted from it by the fire—or more exactly by the threat it posed to Nancy Cronin. Now, riding through the dead land, knowing that this was Clete Yeager's doing, Blaine realized that he wanted to face Yeager as much as Keatch.

Not because of some burned grass. Because of a young woman whose courage had awakened admiration, a young man who was on his back, perhaps even a grudgingly friendly rancher with his back to the wall or a grizzled puncher who was tired of a lead feud. He didn't want to see any of them beaten, forced to quit, or driven to violence they didn't want.

The land was resilient. It would recover, however long
that took. People were more easily crippled or destroyed.

There were many well-meaning folks who believed that a
certain amount of sorrow and adversity were necessary and
good for the soul. Blaine did not wholly subscribe to that
notion. All too often adversity was simply destructive, and
suffering crippled mind and body and spirit. Hard-scrabble
poverty did not always ennoble. It was more likely to make
the spirit mean, the body stunted, the mind twisted into bitterness and envy. There were blows that could not be en-
dured without something being permanently destroyed,
losses that could never be replaced.

Blaine knew how a loss could change a man. He was not
the same man he had been before Samantha's death. It was
hard even to remember what had been in his mind back
then. Plans, dreams. Love for a woman, and thoughts of a
son and of all the things a man might do with his son. Worry
about the next drive, about the price of beef at the market,
about the winter drift or the spring tally of calves. It had
seemed all-important then, the very fabric of his life and his
future. All of it had ended in one morning, and now it was
like it had never been. Now his purposes were narrower,
more limited. Now he did not look much beyond his next
goal, the next man he had to find. He dreamed no dreams.

Restlessly Blaine shrugged off the drift of these thoughts.
He was aware that he had allowed the valley's fight to become his own, in spite of his denial of involvement. But all
that had really changed was that he had added another man
to the list of those he hunted. What Yeager had done could
not be ignored. He was of the same stamp as Keatch and the
others.

He thought of Nancy Cronin, and of the look of ardent
purpose in her face when she was tending to Brad Simmons
after he was helped into her bunkhouse. Perhaps all those
two needed was a chance to be thrown together for a while,
as they surely would be now. Nancy deserved that chance.

She wouldn't have it—not safely—while Clete Yeager was allowed to ride roughshod through the valley, making its war his own.

When he neared the foothills, Blaine swung north, following the stream to the point where it emerged from the mouth of a canyon. Here a trail wound upward through steep-faced bluffs, bordering the stream bed which, over countless centuries, had cut its path through the solid rock.

Blaine regarded the trail dubiously. A camp at the head of this canyon might have been chosen strategically because it couldn't be approached in secret. And the bottom of a canyon was no place to be caught by a pair of waiting gunmen.

Still, he had little choice. According to Nancy Cronin this was the only direct route to her line shack. Any other way would take him on a long encirclement. It seemed unlikely that Yeager—if indeed he had come to the shack to meet Ned Keatch, as Blaine was guessing—would linger there. Time argued against any delay. Moreover, he had the advantage that there was no reason for either Yeager or Keatch to be expecting him now.

With some continuing skepticism, Blaine turned Randy's head along the trail into the forbidding ravine.

They climbed steadily. The skies had cleared in the aftermath of the storm, and there was a bright sun that built up heat in the deep chasm and created hard shadows. The air was humid, and Blaine's shirt, so recently drenched, clung to his back where the sweat ran freely. For a while the walls rose higher and steeper, pressing in on Blaine uncomfortably, with the trail little more than a slender track just above the rocky bed of the stream. The ground was hard, and it was impossible to travel over it without having Randy's hoofs ring and clatter off the rock surface. Blaine began to speculate on the wisdom of making the last part of the climb on foot.

At last, to his relief, the walls of the canyon began to break up. More sky showed as the granite cliffs split into huge, irregular formations. Looking ahead, Blaine saw the line that marked the head of the canyon. The shack was near.

He began to look for a way out of the bottom, a place he might climb so that he wouldn't have to approach the shack from below along the open trail.

It was at this moment that he first heard a distant rumbling.

He thought it might be thunder rolling down from the far peaks of the Towers. But it didn't stop, and it grew louder with a swiftness that startled and confused—and then brought the hard alarm of realization.

Blaine saw a steep cut to his left. He dug in his heels and drove Randy toward the cleft. The big horse resisted, for there seemed to be no way to climb through that opening and to rise almost straight up the shaft it created. But then the buckskin reacted to the avalanche of sound descending on them, and he leaped forward with a surge of power and heart.

Horse and rider clawed their way ten feet above the trail before the wall of water came. It was nearly as high as they had climbed, close enough to brush their feet, a raging force that pummeled them with sound and spray as it roared down the canyon.

Fear drove Randy into new efforts. Horse and rider fought upward through the niche in the canyon wall, a way so narrow that Blaine felt rock scraping his legs on either side. Then there was a widening in the cleft. He saw an opening ahead, and he slid from Randy's back, slapping the horse's haunch as he dropped off. Lighter then, his burden shed, the buckskin leaped ahead with Blaine struggling along behind him.

And suddenly the track leveled off and opened out.

Randy bounded onto the flat rock at the rim overlooking the canyon. A moment later Blaine reached the top.

He stood looking down, his chest heaving, stunned and deafened, feeling a deep awe at the fury below him as he watched it smash its way down the ravine. He had been caught in a flash flood once before, but that had been in the open, and although he had been swept along some thirty yards or more he had survived. Nothing caught in the path of this torrent would have survived.

The waters were beginning to recede when a sixth sense warned Blaine that he was not alone.

His glance shot toward the head of the canyon. He had a glimpse of the roof of a shack, but it was not this that caught his eye. Two men were on the rim just above the shack, perhaps driven there as he had been by fear of the sudden flood. And they had been there when Blaine appeared out of the canyon.

He saw this and understood it in that instant of vision. He also saw the shine of sunlight on a long barrel and the spurt of powder smoke.

A burning pain seared his belly. The impact spun him off his feet. He was too near the edge, and he flopped over it, tumbling out of control.

He bounced off rocks and skidded and rolled. Landing on the narrow ledge of the trail he clawed at it, trying to arrest his fall, but there was no strength in his hands, and blackness seized him like a giant fist and pulled him down.

* * *

"I tol' you!" Ned Keatch whined. "I tol' you he wasn't human. You said he was penned up at Rocking Chair, and here he is!"

"I don't know how he got here," Yeager said grimly. "But it don't matter now. He's hit."

"I won't believe it until I see him belly up."

The two men worked their way along the rim overlooking the canyon. Neither wanted to risk going down into the draw after that violent flooding. It might not be the last. The recent cloudburst had been too sudden a torrent to be absorbed in the high mountains. There was no predicting when another wall of water might thunder down between those walls.

"Wasn't for that water, we never would've seen him," Keatch muttered. "He was comin' up, and we would've been sittin' ducks. He must've heard it comin', and that drove him up where we seen him."

"He won't be scarin' folks no more," Clete Yeager said, eying his partner with contempt. Keatch's face was white, a color it had turned in the instant he saw Blaine climb against the skyline. Keatch had been too panicky to pull his gun. It was Yeager whose shot had dropped Blaine.

"Where is he?" Keatch said. "Damn it, there's his horse. Where the hell did he go?"

Yeager did not answer. Six-gun in his hand, he approached the buckskin cautiously, but he had no doubt that Blaine had gone over the side. The only question was how badly he had been hit. The shot had been quick. There was no time for careful aiming.

He saw the steep slash through which Blaine had incredibly climbed out of the canyon to escape the flood waters. Carefully Yeager inched up to the rim and peered over.

His breath hissed softly. After a moment he said, "You can stop shakin' in your boots, Keatch. There's your hellion down there."

Ned Keatch scurried forward quickly to stare down into the canyon. His heart thumped. Relief came with such force that he began to shake. Yeager watched him, thinking with disgust that this was the fierce gunman he had been going to ride with into a war. Yet, mingled with the contempt, there was also some puzzlement. Blaine was a hard man to keep down, obviously, but he had not proved to be so awesome as to inspire the kind of fear Ned Keatch had been living with.

Blaine lay on his back at the bottom of the ravine, one leg in the water. The stream was running higher than normal after the flash flood, boiling over its rocky bed. Another roll and Blaine would have been head down in the water, Yeager speculated. But it didn't seem to matter one way or the other. His broken sprawl seemed to say enough, but there was something else that brought a grin to Yeager's lips. Blaine had been gut shot.

"By God, that's him, all right," Keatch said, his voice trembling with either fear or hatred.

"He won't bother you no more."

"I gotta be sure. You don't know him."

"I can see he took that bullet in the belly," Yeager said with satisfaction. "If he isn't dead yet, he'll soon be wishin' he was." Even at this distance the evidence was plain. Blaine's jeans were red over his belly. There was no worse wound, as far as Yeager was concerned. "You can climb down there if you want, but not me. I won't risk bein' caught by another flood, not for a dead man."

"Well, I'm makin' sure of him," Keatch blurted, taking aim at the prone figure in the canyon bottom. But his hand still shook and he swore aloud.

Then a distant rumbling made him pause. He looked at Yeager, and both men stared in the direction of the sound. There was only a moment or two of waiting before they knew that what they heard was the same fury that had brought them up on the heights a short while ago, in time to see Cullom Blaine appear like a ghost rising from the ground.

Keatch looked down anxiously. Just as his finger squeezed the trigger the water came with a rush. It washed over Blaine's body as Keatch fired.

The flash flood was shallower than the earlier one, and in

seconds it was gone down the canyon, leaving behind a deeper river that frothed white. The two men stared down.

The canyon bottom was empty. Cullom Blaine was gone.

NINETEEN

Ned Keatch caught the trailing reins of Blaine's buckskin, which followed him, tossing his head nervously. Yeager led the way back toward the line shack, his face turned ahead so that Keatch could not see the speculation in his eyes. Conversationally Yeager said, "I'll be gettin' back to the Rocking Chair. If the boys caught Simmons out the way they was supposed to, there'll be hell to pay from some of those Association hotheads. I'll be ready for 'em . . . and after today they'll curl up their tails and crawl away."

Keatch heard the satisfaction in Yeager's voice, the undercurrent of triumph. It was early to be celebrating, he thought. "What about me?" he said.

Yeager hesitated a moment, not looking back, as if he were seriously pondering the question. Then he said, "I'm thinkin' you oughta put this valley behind you, Keatch. You got nothin' to keep you here now. If you stick, it'll come out that you switched sides while you were workin' for Paradise. Once that gets noised around, your life won't be worth any more than Blaine's is now. The Association might be whipped, but some of those hired gunslicks won't take it kindly that you worked both sides."

"You figurin' to pay me off now?" Keatch asked softly.

"That's right. . . ." Yeager swung around casually, his shoulders loose and ready. He found himself looking along the barrel of Keatch's gun. "What the hell—!"

There was a tight, malicious grin on the little gunman's face. His bright pop eyes had an odd glitter, hardly sane.

"You think I didn't know what you was fixin' to do?" he said.

"Don't be a damned fool!" Yeager felt a cold inner fury, raging at himself for his mistake. He had allowed his contempt for Keatch to make him careless, forgetting for the moment that a cowardly man with a quick gun was the most dangerous kind, untrustworthy and unpredictable. "I brought your pay—you got no complaint."

"Then I'll just taken it off you, 'stead of havin' you pocket it all for yourself. You had it in mind all along to shut me up, I reckon."

"Listen to me, Keatch, you've got it wrong. You can leave now that Blaine's dead. You're no worry to me out of this valley, and you'll be safe."

"I wouldn't be safe turnin' my back on you," Keatch insisted doggedly, as if this were an earnest discussion. "You don't need me no more, but you wouldn't want me alive to talk about what happened at Paradise in the spring . . . or how Sean Roark was double-crossed. Ain't no use pretendin' other, Yeager."

"Damn it, Keatch, you grabbed the wrong end of the stick, I swear!"

He had to make his move then, the only one left to him. Keatch was just crazy enough and sly enough to have guessed what he had planned. Fear had kept Keatch from acting while Blaine lived and he wanted help, but that weight was off his back now. Yeager hadn't expected him to strike so soon, that was all. He had been congratulating himself on his own decision to cut Keatch down when he swung around to look into the muzzle of the little gunman's .44 Colt.

Yeager threw himself to the side as his hand struck for the gun at his hip. It was a desperate gamble and it never had a chance.

The gun in Keatch's hand bucked. Yeager saw the barrel tip upward. Everything was slow, like moving in molasses.

The sound expanded slowly, a roaring that swelled until it filled his ears. He knew that his hand had reached the butt of his gun and that his finger had squeezed the trigger, but the barrel never cleared the holster. The bullet burned leather and ricocheted off rock. Then he was falling back, and pain opened like a flower in his chest, slowly, until it merged with the roaring and there was nothing else.

For Ned Keatch, watching, it did not happen slowly at all. The .44 slug fired at point-blank range bowed Yeager's body out like a boot in the belly. He flopped backward, did a funny dance as if he were on stilts, and went down screaming. Even the scream was short.

Keatch walked over to him and prodded the body with his toe. He watched the stain spread over Yeager's shirt. After a moment he bared his teeth and holstered his gun.

He found less than twenty dollars in Yeager's pockets, and was so enraged that he kicked the dead man viciously. He'd been right! Yeager never meant to pay him his wages at all.

When he calmed down, Keatch heard a rubbing sound behind him and whirled in dry-mouthed apprehension. It was only Blaine's buckskin, but Keatch's heart continued to hammer. For an instant he had thought . . .

He had to be sure, Keatch thought. It was all right for Yeager to shrug off Blaine's chances of surviving a gut shot and a canyon flood. Keatch wouldn't finally believe it until he found Blaine lying stiff and cold. Then he could stop jumping at every sound. Then he could breathe freely at last.

He left the buckskin in the little pole corral by the line shack. Then, walking gingerly and cautiously, Keatch started down the canyon trail.

TWENTY

Blaine waited.

He knew that, sooner or later, Keatch would come. He would have to make sure. He wouldn't be able to let it go.

Blaine did not pay attention to his condition, but certain facts were crucial. He could move both arms and legs. He had dislocated a finger on his bandaged hand, but he had snapped it back into place. The bleeding which had soaked his jeans had stopped. The wound had been cleansed and the blood aided in coagulating by the deep chill of the water.

He had been looking into the canyon when Clete Yeager fired at him. Blaine had turned only his head, and his body had presented only a side view to Yeager. The bullet had plowed a shallow furrow across his belly. The burning sensation had been bad for a while, but the fear had been worse. The amount of bleeding had been shocking.

Blaine was just as glad he hadn't seen it at first. Tumbling down the face of the cliff and into the bed of the stream, he had cracked his head on a rock and lost consciousness. The spill of icy mountain water—the second such flooding in a span of minutes—had awakened him as it washed him downstream. This was not as deep or powerful as the first flash flood, but it might still have banged him up dangerously as it rolled him down the canyon. Luckily, the first wash had carried him only a few feet, driving him under a ledge and between two big rocks with enough force to wedge him there.

In seconds the torrent had disappeared down the ravine.

Blaine lay where he was, awake then, but unable to move, half in and half out of the deeper river that continued to flow. He had become aware of the bleeding then, of the river running red, but he supposed now that there hadn't been as much blood as it appeared.

After a while, when he figured that he could cope with the slower surge of the stream without being washed downhill, he had wriggled out of the fissure in which he had been pinned. Looking up, he realized that he could not be seen from above. The outcropping of rock at the edge of the trail concealed him.

He heard a single shot.

His first jolting thought was that Keatch or Yeager was shooting at him again. After a moment he realized that this didn't make sense. Besides, the shot had come from some distance up the canyon.

Trying to make sense of it, the only thing Blaine could come up with was a falling out of thieves. Perhaps Yeager felt that he didn't need Keatch any more. Or perhaps it was the other way around, and it was Keatch who had caught Yeager by surprise, acting for reasons Blaine could not fathom.

It was this possibility that kept him anchored where he was, just under the lip of rock, playing possum as he waited for Keatch—if he was still alive—to come and verify that he was finished. Blaine was out of the water, but he had two persistent worries other than Keatch or Yeager. One was the possibility that another flood would sweep him away. There was nothing he could do about that without showing himself. The other concern was that the bullets in his Colt would misfire. He shook them out of the cylinder, dried them as well as he could (there was nothing dry about him other than his breath and the rub of his fingers), and stuffed them back in the chambers. He wouldn't know until the moment came whether or not one cartridge—or more—might fail.

He heard a tick of sound.

Stiffening, Blaine kept his eye on a small patch of the trail visible to him through a gap in the rocks. He couldn't risk lifting his head to see more.

A light scraping. Someone approached cautiously on tip-toe.

Blaine's eyes watered from staring, and he blinked away the moisture. His vision cleared just in time to see a pair of boots below skinny legs flick across that little patch of trail that was in his line of vision. He had no chance to get off a shot that would do any real harm.

The man drew closer, his careful steps more clearly audible, whispering across the rock ledge that served as a trail. He came abreast of Blaine, hesitated just above him, and moved on.

Very slowly Blaine twisted his body around so that he could face downstream. About ten yards below him, the entire trail came into view. Blaine lifted his Colt and sighted on that open space. He had to hold the gun in his left hand, but he steadied it with his right.

Ned Keatch shuffled into sight.

Blaine knew instantly that it had to be Keatch. No stranger would have been so desperate to make sure of him. The figure was much too short and thin to be Yeager. He had slope shoulders and a narrow back. Like Blaine now, he was hatless. His hair was the color of the granite walls of the canyon. His gun was in his hand.

The figure stopped, like an animal sensing danger, pausing to sniff the air.

"Here, Keatch," Blaine called out softly. "Behind you."

Keatch jerked around. Blaine's finger squeezed and the hammer fell with a hollow snap, striking a dud cartridge. In the same moment Keatch fired.

The distance was so short that the gunman never should have missed. It was a panic shot, however, fired at a ghost, a

man who was still alive when he had no right to be. The
bullet slapped the rock ledge under which Blaine had been
lying. He felt the sting of rock spray on his cheek as he
pulled the trigger a second time. He was aiming carefully,
steadying the Colt with both hands, and the shot struck
Keatch squarely in the chest. He bounced off the canyon
wall and dropped into the churning stream. It carried him
out of sight.

Blaine lay back wearily. There was no feeling of satisfaction, only a strange, sudden emptiness.

* * *

In the late afternoon Cullom Blaine rode slowly across the
wide bench toward the headquarters of the Rocking Chair.
By the time he reached the outbuildings the area was more
crowded than he had seen it before. It was also strangely silent.

Blaine saw Kate Roark emerge from the house. She
remained on the porch, staring at him as he approached
slowly.

He rode within a dozen feet of the porch before he pulled
up. Clete Yeager's horse, trailing behind, stopped when he
did. The horse stood uncertainly, shifting weight a little
restlessly, uneasy with the lifeless burden draped across the
saddle. Blaine had not retrieved Keatch's body from the
canyon, but he had a hunch that it was important for the
Rocking Chair crew to see Yeager.

In a toneless voice Blaine said, "I figured you might want
to bury him."

"You needn't have bothered. Walden told me what you
said about . . . about him and my father. Is it true, Mr.
Blaine?"

"I reckon we won't never know for certain."

"It's true," she said dully. "I should have seen it before."

Blaine shrugged. "It was true about Keatch. Yeager hired him while he was supposed to be workin' for Paradise. He was there when that fire started in the spring, and he's been hidin' out since. Yeager was the only one knew where he was all this time, I reckon, although some of your other hands rode with Keatch recently."

"We didn't know about burnin' down the Cronin place," someone called out behind Blaine. "Nor about Yeager and Roark."

Blaine didn't turn. He knew from the sound of that voice that the heart had been cut out of the Rocking Chair crew. If any had still been eager to fight, seeing Yeager stretched across his saddle had ended it. The men who had been hired for their guns would be drifting on soon.

He said, "I reckon you'll want to see him buried all the same."

"Not on this land," Kate Roark said, with a trace of the vibrancy in her voice that Blaine was accustomed to hearing. "Will you attend to it, Walden?"

"Yes, ma'am."

A question, Blaine mused, not an order. He looked at her closely. Her face was drawn, but if anything that only served to make her more beautiful. One thing, however, was missing: that haughty, arrogant pride. She seemed very vulnerable, and Blaine almost pitied her.

"I'll be leavin', then."

He was turning Randy's head when Kate Roark called out. "Mr. Blaine! That . . . that offer I made you. It's still good. You don't have to leave."

He sat for a moment, not moving. He was bone tired and his whole body ached. It would have been good to climb down and rest awhile.

But he still had the strength to nudge the buckskin with his knees. They set off, walking slowly away from the house. Blaine thought of the big old spruce under which he had bedded down his first night in the Antelope Valley. He might crawl under that tree again, he thought, and hibernate like a bear.

He did not look back.